WILLIAM PRICE'S

LITERARY ODYSSEY

A novella by

Mervyn Matthews

By the same author

Mila and Mervusya (1999)
Mervyn's Lot (2002)
(Seren Books, Bridgend)

Mother Russia (2008)
Mervyn's Russia (2009)
(Hodgson Press, Surbiton)

WILLIAM PRICE'S

LITERARY ODYSSEY

A novella by

Mervyn Matthews

Hodgson Press

First published in Great Britain by Hodgson Press 2009

Hodgson Press
PO Box 903^A
Kingston upon Thames
Surrey
KT1 9LY
United Kingdom
enquiries@hodgsonpress.co.uk
www.hodgsonpress.co.uk

Copyright © Mervyn Matthews, 2009

All rights reserved. No part of this publication may be reproduced, stored in a retrieval system, or transmitted, in any form, or by any means, without the prior permission in writing of Hodgson Press, or as expressly permitted by law, or under terms agreed with the appropriate reprographics rights organization. Enquiries concerning reproduction outside the scope of the above should be sent to Hodgson Press at the above address. Illustrations copyright of their copyright holders.

The moral right of the author has been asserted.

You must not circulate this book in any other binding or cover and you must impose this condition on any acquirer.

A CIP catalogue record for this book is available from the British Library.

ISBN: 978-1-906164-07-2

Printed in Great Britain by Lightning Source Ltd.

Contents

FOREWORD ix

Part I

ST. STEPHEN'S PARISH NEWSLETTER	3
William Writes to Maisie	4
William Writes to Rosalinda Press	5
DO NOT UNTO OTHERS	6
The Vicar's Wife Complains (a note by hand)	10
… And William Replies	11
A Letter from the Publisher	12
DIARY – Life Without Maisie	13
William Tries Again	16
A Letter From Mildred Oates, Rosalinda secretary	18
DIARY – The Trials of Life	19
A Letter to Eric in Australia	20
William Tries another Publisher	21
Mr. Boxer Writes a Nice Letter	22
1770 PACIFIC DRIVE (Publisher's Outline)	23
Mr. Boxer Writes an Interesting Letter	27
DIARY – William Gets Good News	28
Another Letter to Penarth	30
Maisie Worries a Little	31
DIARY – Trouble at the Shop	33
A Really Nice Publisher	37
William Makes Arrangements	38
Note to Alistair	39
DIARY – The Publisher's Lunch	40
William Writes to Maisie	44
… And to Eric	45
A Word of Advice	47

Part II

A Police Report	51
A Letter from Sunrise Assurance, Ltd	53
… And the Coop Bank	54
DIARY – The Big Sales Day	55
The Publisher's Advance	60
Letter to Carmarthen Caravans, Ltd.	61
Maisie Reassured	62
Alistair's Billet Doux	64
DIARY – Night thoughts	65
Another Note to Alistair	67
The Rosalinda Young Authors Competition	68
The Vicar Complains Again	69
… And William Replies	70
DIARY – Father and Son	71
Some Bad News for Maisie	73
Maisie Gets Worked up Again	75
Rosalinda Publishers Write to Alistair	76
SHE DONE HER BIT	77
Maisie Gives Instructions	79
Carmarthen Caravans Responds	81
Mr. Boxer Once More	82
Can Eric Help?	84
Eat a Friend!	85
Rosalinda Press Once More	87
Alistair Despairs – a note	88
To Alistair at Auntie Florrie's	89
Another Nice Letter to Maisie	90
From Head Office, Wilkinson's Furnishings	92

Part III

Charlie French Makes a Suggestion	97
A Letter to a Solicitor	99
Eric Backs Off	100
Neighbourly Interest	101
More Legal Matters	102
DIARY – Tea with Doris	104
William Turns to Eric Again	106
Alistair's Solution	108
Mr. Boxer's New Proposal	109
DIARY – Watery Surprises	110
A Letter of Explanation	113
Alistair Writes to his Mum	115
ST. STEPHEN'S PARISH NEWSLETTER	116
News from Australia	118
DIARY – An Evening at the Cocked Hat	119
The Solicitor Again	121
DIARY – A Visit to the Library	122
Another Police Operation	124
Nora Thorpe writes to the Teckley Argus	126
William Triumphans	127
A Mystery Solved	131
Good News for Maisie	132
Alistair Straightens Out	134
More Motherly Worries	135
Congratulations from on High	137
ST. STEPHEN'S PARISH NEWSLETTER	139

FOREWORD

The various writings which make up this slim volume, dear reader, need a word of explanation. They are intended to illustrate the path which I, William Price, furniture salesman, now in my fiftieth year, trod through the tedious by-ways of publishers' refusals to the happy appearance of my small autobiographical masterpiece entitled '*A Swansea Boyhood*'. All the events described below took place while my dear wife Maisie was out visiting her mother and sister in Australia, leaving our son Alistair and myself at home. My path to authorial eminence was rendered even thornier by family problems (mainly in the shape of Alistair), falsehood, felony, and threat of financial ruin. I am fortunate indeed that a certain presence of mind, and agility of pen, allowed me to surmount all difficulties as they showered upon me. The volume originally went on sale per favor of Larehall Press at the modest price of £9.50, and this being no less than the third impression.

Though I have not, as a consequence of publishing '*Boyhood*', been able to leave the employ of Wilkinson's Furnishings, Ltd., nor move beyond the confines of my domicile at 17, Acacia Crescent, I cherish my success and feel I still have a creative future before me. Having overcome a certain hesitation about the subscription, I have joined the Society of Authors.

As you read on, you may wonder how I managed to bring together so diverse a collection of texts. The writing wholly pre-dated common usage of computers and e-mails – people in my world had to communicate by letter and (expensive) telephone. This is advantageous in so far as it may be more easily remembered or filed away. As for letters, I have the strange habit of keeping both carbon copies of those I dispatch and the originals of those I receive. A few of my occasional notes I was able to retrieve, once I made my literary intentions clear to the recipients. In a few cases I have reproduced the content from memory. The reader will find many extracts from a diary that I kept, since I have long had aspirations as a latter-day Samuel Pepys. One official item was kindly copied from police files by Police Sergeantwoman Copplestone, who at that time liaised with the Acacia Neighbourhood Watch. Other items were culled from the local newspapers. The materials as collected may not be quite complete, but will allow the intelligent reader to comprehend the main events in their proper order.

I hope that the re-publication of these pages will not only make interesting reading, but also encourage those who would be warriors of the pen, honest souls ready to fight for publication and confront head-on the bloody-mindedness of this country's publishing houses.

William Price

17 Acacia Crescent

Teckley.

Part I

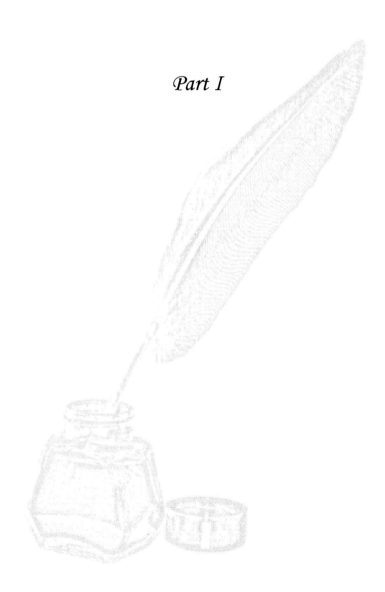

ST. STEPHEN'S PARISH NEWSLETTER

25th February, 1992

Editor: Mrs. Nora Thorpe

"From Day to Day"

Parishioners will be sorry to learn that we shall be losing the enthusiastic help of Mrs. Maisie Price for at least three months. Many of the old folk whom she visited will miss those delicious apple turnovers she always brings, cooked at home in Acacia Crescent! Maisie is off to visit her mother and her sister Conny and family in Australia. We all wish her a good journey – and a safe return to St. Stephen's, hopefully in time for our Christmas services.

...

William Writes to Maisie

28th February, 1992

Dear Maisie,

It was quite a wrench seeing you off on Thursday, and an eerie experience hearing your voice over the phone 24 hours later. A pity the calls cost so much, but Alistair and I will make it up with letters.

Everything is fine here, and a few of the neighbours already asked how you got off. The house will be well looked after. The main thing is for you to have a marvellous, relaxed holiday. I have pinned your list of do's and don'ts up in the kitchen. The vicar called this morning and said if disaster strikes all we have to do is telephone his faithful spouse Nora, she will come over and have a nose around (although he did not put it that way). I think he's desperate to get her out of the house, I would be. Don't worry, garden, laundry, dishes, etc., will all be looked after, and Alistair has promised to be exceptionally helpful, and keep his bedroom clean. I will not forget to lock up when I go out.

I hope the family liked the presents – warmest regards to all. It'll be Alistair's turn to write next.

    Love,

        William.

William Writes to Rosalinda Press

1ˢᵗ March 1992

Dear Mr. Franklin,

I am writing to ask whether your Publishing House has yet come to a decision on the jaunty autobiographical manuscript I submitted five months ago. I am likely to have more time available for creative work this summer, including revision and correction of proofs. I hope you liked it.

I had a superb idea for a novel while doing the rockery yesterday evening, an outline of which I also enclose for your careful perusal. If published, it will need to be done so under a pseudonym, so as not to offend certain religious connections.

I look forward to hearing from you as soon as may be convenient.

Yours sincerely,

William Price

DO NOT UNTO OTHERS

A novel, by William Price, [Outline]

"Do not unto others as you would have them do unto you: they may not like it" (Bernard Shaw)

Clarence Taunton is a skilled balloonist and part-time lecturer in female hygiene at Smithfield Polytechnic. Though he failed to complete a course in medicine he is a studious type, well aware of the benefits of learning. He has an interest in archaeology. The reader also learns that he is a bachelor in his mid forties.

His cultural interests prompt him, one August, to join a tourist group bound for Palestine. The plot of the novel effectively starts one blazing hot afternoon when the group is going around the ramparts in Caeseria. Clarence slips behind a ruined wall in order better to view the terrain for a possible balloon ascent later in the year: there are a number of enthusiasts at the poly. His intelligent gaze falls from the blue sky to the dusty and cracked masonry, wherein he perceives a half-buried pot. He quickly removes it, breaks open the wax seal, and lights upon some ancient scrolls. These startling actions take but a few minutes.

He is a fairly experienced traveller, and never goes anywhere without a couple of Salisbury plastic bags in his pocket (you never know when they will come in handy). He carefully places the urn in one of them. Back in the bus some of the more curious members of the group ask him what he has found. With characteristic wit he announces that he has found the tit of a crumbling Roman goddess, which he intends to cement into the middle of his mantelpiece at home, or use for demonstration purposes in class…

That evening, back at the German Sisters' Hospice in Haifa, he takes a closer look at his find. The Hospice was rather full, so the German Sisters dumped him in that awful outhouse at the back, and he has no immediate neighbours. He spreads out bits of the scroll on the rickety Weimar table, and since many years previously he had started, but not finished, an O-level course in Aramaic, soon realises that the fragments are written precisely in that ancient tongue.

He is very excited about the find and wants to get to the bottom of it himself. So he puts the pot and its contents in his suitcase and takes it back to England, deciding that any legal complications about exporting antiques can be sorted out by the Law Department at the poly.

[NB. If the Publishers wished to give the story an even more racy, and at once earthy coloration, I could here introduce a sub-plot centred on Clarence's brother George. George is a ballistics expert who also joins the tourist group, and after the visit, with the best humanitarian intentions, starts work on a deadly accurate sleaze gun for use against juvenile rioters on the West Bank, (instead of the fire arms and tear gas normally used). The weapon would be designed to fire a revolting mixture of camel shit, vomit and rancid butter, the main technical problem being to stop the mixture spreading after it leaves the barrel, and maintain it in large blobs over long distances. Apart from the Israelis, the South African and Chinese intelligence groups find out about it (since they share electronic eavesdropping facilities at the German Sisters). Having in mind possible uses in Soweto and Tibet they start competing amongst themselves over surveillance, and shadow Clarence and George in the street.]

Anyway, over the next few months Clarence revises his Aramaic and starts translating the scrolls. He also has them perused, in great secrecy, by an Oxbridge Professor of Hebrew, a Keeper of Ancient Manuscripts at the British Museum, an unemployed Ph. D. in Semitic philology and three Church of England Bible Bishops. Finally he gets the scrolls carbon-dated in the polytechnic laboratory.

The findings are together irrefutable: he has found Jesus Christ's original diary.

At this point of acute suspense the novel develops two threads (unless the riot gun is added at the Publisher's request and makes a third). The first concerns Clarence's efforts to get the diary published. He has it translated into beautifully balanced prose and sends it off to Croom Helm, who at first lose it then return it with a curt letter of refusal. It appears that they get on average ten unsolicited manuscripts a day, and do not normally read them. Clarence compiles a list of sixty four publishers who all refuse, leaving our hero in despair. His performance at the poly suffers badly, and the feminist group among the staff even call for his dismissal. He is almost expelled from the balloon club for negligent inflation.

The second thread springs from the fact that the diary contains some nasty insinuations about Moses, and evidence that Islam was around long before Mohammed got there. No one knows about this until one of the Bible Bishops gets drunk at an ecumenical gathering and spills the beans. Unfortunately, some Fundamental Moslems and Militant Synagogians overhear him and hatch various devilish plots to steal the originals, so that they may be censored, cut, and re-interpreted. (If necessary, the intelligence groups can be brought back into the plot here to thicken it).

The last scene of the novel takes place in the basket of a balloon above Lambeth Bridge, watched by a crowd of office workers causing a monumental traffic jam. There are also a few surgeons on their way to do operations in Westminster Hospital. Clarence, having despaired of publication, and learnt about the various plots to seize the scrolls, decided to have an absolutely exclusive auction among interested parties. The Archbishop of Canterbury, the Chief Rabbi and the Imam of Bradford are in the basket with him bidding, together with a skinny (i.e. relatively light) solicitor. The latter is there to record the transaction. (If necessary, the various intelligence groups can be hovering around, infuriated, in helicopters). The bidding goes wrong and a fight ensues; the Imam has his turban knocked off, the Rabbi is done a physical mischief, and the Archbishop of Canterbury loses his false teeth in the Thames. Clarence manages to bring the balloon safely down off Westminster Pier, and medical assistance is provided by the surgeons.

The whole affair now gets into the papers; Clarence becomes rich and famous from the astute sale of bits of his story, and has to avoid the attentions of well-known publishers in Soho restaurants.

The end.

The Vicar's Wife Complains (a note by hand)
                                                    3rd March 1992

Dear Mr. Price,

Do excuse this note so soon after Maisie left. But as you know – a stitch in time…

Last night Alistair seems to have had a party. At least, there was light in your loft conversion till after three, and the noise was terrible. Cigarette ends and, disgustingly, a used rubberoid item were tossed onto our lawn. The vicar and I are surprised you let it go on so long. Maisie as an active member of our congregation would hardly have approved. After all, the early hours also are the Sabbath, which is my husband's heavy day in the pulpit.

We hope this will not develop into a pattern, or attract undesirable attention to our quiet road.

Sincerely,

Nora Thorpe

... And William Replies

3rd March 1992

Dear Mrs. Thorpe,

Both Alistair and I apologise for the noise last night. Things did get a bit out of hand later on, and I had to intervene myself. Alistair has promised to be very helpful while his mother is away, but he had some of his friends from the Polytechnic along to celebrate the end of their exams. Perhaps the cigarette ends came from another direction, Maisie would be most upset to hear it. With regard to the rubberoid item, please bear in mind the proximity of the chemist's. Many devoted married couples must admire your lawn while on a discrete journey to the surgical goods counter. Intimacy is much more adventurous than it used to be, and before casting aspersions you might look for tell-tale signs in the turf – flattened grass and indentations. I'm surprised it hasn't happened before.

While writing, may I say that buying a peacock to beautify the vicarage lawn was a lovely idea. But is there any way of stopping it screeching at dawn? Miss Crosby also complains. Also, If your dear daughter Celia could modify her language when third persons are in earshot, I would be most grateful. I would not have thought that a few weeds could provoke such appalling utterance.

Maisie arrived safely, and, when she phoned, asked to be remembered to you.

Yours sincerely,

W. P.

A Letter from the Publisher

13th March 1992

Dear Mr. Price,

Thank you for your letters of 4th October and the 1st March.

I have now had a chance to consider both your autobiography and your outline "Do not unto others". I am sorry to disappoint you, but we don't feel that either is something for Rosalinda Press. I really think the best thing for you to do would be to find a literary agent to take an interest in your projects, perhaps in the Metropolis.

With best wishes for your writing this summer.

Yours sincerely,

Andrew Franklin, Executive Editor

P.S. I'm afraid I cannot respond to the suggestion in your February letter that my firm invite you to a "publisher's lunch" for discussion of your text. Personally, I do not have the time, apart from which our entertainment budget is limited to meals for seasoned authors of long standing.

DIARY – *Life Without Maisie*

15th March 1992

Life rolls on as usual. I regard myself as a comfortably settled man, but I certainly have my problems. The main one is Maisie: there's nothing nasty there, but she exudes a fussiness, a concern with domestic triviality, which is most wearing for anyone of literary inclination (like myself). If she had her way I don't suppose I would write a word. Life is much more relaxed when she is not here. God knows how she would react if she knew that Alistair's friends cracked the bedroom ceiling when he had the party a few nights ago. It was all the dancing in the loft conversion. Tolstoy, I believe, had problems with his spouse, and died running away from her. But he had something to be thankful for as well, I could hardly imagine Maisie copying "War and Peace" twice.

Then there's all this church business. Being friendly with the vicar means I get drawn into it myself a bit, and even go to listen to the occasional sermon, and help fill a pew for him. But if the truth be told, Sunday School in Swansea put me off religion for life. The worse thing about St. Stephen's is that it seems to have totally blighted Maisie's interest in sex. The sight of her "respectable" flannelette bloomers would have made Casanova's member wilt. The same goes for her "serviceable" nighties. And Alistair's constant escapades with attractive young females don't make me feel any better. Good luck to him, I suppose.

My work at Wilkinson's Furniture Emporium on High Street is unbelievably boring. I was never cut out for selling furniture. Today I wasted half the morning trying to sell a double bed - arguing about metal springs is not an inspiring activity.

In Acacia Avenue - a mass of trivialities. Arrived home to find that Pinkey had got into the fridge and eaten the cockles I was defrosting for tea (I like them with fresh bread and butter). Alistair must have left the door open again. For some reason this reminded me that we had not written to Maisie. Decided to give her a quick ring, and found she was furious we had not done so. A minute and a half was rather too long. She was also strangely curious about what might be going on, in fact I am wondering whether Nora Thorpe has been writing to her behind our backs. Probably not, because Maisie didn't know Alistair had bleached his hair.

Telephoned Jack Marples about repairing the ceiling. Even without seeing it he thought it would cost two hundred pounds. He's coming with his mate next week. I told him I wanted a faint off-pink hue, to go with the curtains. Maisie would like it. It was partly my fault, I should have put a limit on the number of people Alistair took up, or stopped the dancing sooner.

Anyway, yesterday I made him spend the evening with me cutting the lawn and trimming the hedge by way of penance. In fact he had spoilt the shears cutting brass stars for his new motorbike. I can't imagine where he got the money to buy it, and I thought it better not to ask. The rhododendron looked ropey, so I chucked a couple of buckets of water over it. It revived visibly. Alistair did Heinz beans on toast for supper, quite nice, I must say. Perhaps he'll go into catering when he finishes at the poly, something on the managerial side. But his English is terrible, he seems incapable of distinguishing between standard utterance and this dreadful student slang. I think he started doing it on purpose to annoy me, and he can't get out of it now.

One bright spot, perhaps. I telephoned a prestigious London literary agent and the girl on the telephone said I might do better in Wales, in fact she gave me the number of a publishing house in Penarth called Bristol Channel Press. When I rang them, the telephone was answered by a child who intimated that the manager, a Mr. Boxer, was away on an ornithological trip (watching birdies in the scrub, I think she said). A mature-sounding lady then took the instrument and introduced herself as his niece Doris. They are apparently reopening a long-standing family publishing business specialising in spiritual values, Anglo-Welsh literature and shellfish, though they take anything that might sell. The Principal has been away and is due to return some weeks hence. It sounds promising, and she said she could pass on any letters. Apart from publishing they do a side-line in holiday breaks for distressed authors in Wales. Maisie would like that, though we have the caravan, anyway. I arranged to send them some outlines.

Also just sent off another idea to Rosalinda Press, one has to keep trying.

I am sure Pinkey is pregnant again.

William Tries Again

15th March 1992

Dear Mr. Franklin,

Thank you for your letter of the 13th March instant. Despite, however, the disappointments so far, I presume your House is always interested in creative ideas. I have had another, pursuance of which would possibly be better than rewriting my autobiography, or even "Do not unto others". May I set it out in a little more detail?

In fact it came to me some time ago, last summer, when my wife and I were visiting the Ufficial Galleries in Florence. It was rather tiring, not least because my lady wife complained that her neck ached from looking up at the ceilings. When we got to Michelangelo's statue of the David of Milan which stands outside, however, our gaze was directed downwards, and a striking idea occurred to me. What is the most literally neglected part of that young fellow's anatomy? On picture postcards, I mean? The noble brow? The fine shoulders? The splendid torso? His honest dangles? No, reproductions of all can be bought for a few lira. But what about his <u>feet</u>?

I wonder whether Rosalinda would be interested in an illustrated coffee-table book entitled something like "The Foot in History"? The pictures could go through from the earliest cave drawings to (say) some of the Royal Family's toes (which I am sure have been photographed somewhere). We could include captions with verses from the Messiah ('How beautiful are the feet') or the revelations of selected Harley Street chiropodists. Did you know that Lenin was once photographed in enormous clodhoppers? The content of this volume would need a lot of thought, and if you are interested I would be grateful for suggestions.

Re your earlier suggestion about engaging a literary agent, I rang Curtiss Brown (who I gather are very famous), but was told that Mr. Brown was not available to come to the phone. In the end a girl in the office gave me the number of a firm outside Penarth, who, she heard, deals in manuscripts. It doesn't seem a very likely spot to me, but I will pursue it.

I am grateful for your interest, and look forward to your responses on the foot.

  Yours sincerely,

  William Price.

P.S. It occurred to me that if you have no time for a publisher's lunch perhaps you could accept my invitation to a special tea in the Ritz. My wife was taken there two years ago, and she said the atmosphere is very conducive to creative discussion. Of course, I would need to know a few days in advance to arrange time off from my place of employment. The shop I work for closes early on Thursdays.

A Letter From Mildred Oates, Rosalinda secretary
25th March, 1992

Dear Mr. Price,

Mr. Franklin has asked me to reply to your letter of the 15th March. Unfortunately your idea for a coffee-table book about feet does not seem viable to him, and he will not be available for tea at any establishment in the foreseeable future. He still strongly feels that you would do better to work through a literary agent, a list of whom can be found in the Writers and Artists Yearbook.

It has never been our policy to discourage would-be authors, but Mr. Franklin feels, frankly, that the material you have sent would not be touched with the proverbial bargepole by most. He added, (in a jocular manner, of course) that a publisher would have to be dyslexic to consider it.

Good luck in your efforts,

    Yours Sincerely,

        Mildred Oates.
        p.p. A. Franklin.

DIARY – *The Trials of Life*

28th March 1992

You would think that in a spot like Acacia Crescent nothing much happened and we all lived in peace and quite. I suppose a diarist should be happy that things are not thus, though it is true that excessive activity can destroy the simple creature comforts essential to good writing. Especially if he is robbed of a night's sleep!

At two a.m. I was awakened by the sound of someone trying to force the dining room window downstairs. Thoroughly perturbed, I decided to investigate, before calling the police. It turned out to be Alistair, who had forgotten his keys, and was trying to get in without ringing the doorbell. I was just dropping off to sleep again when my ear caught the chink of a garden spade hitting bits of stone. I jumped to the bedroom window. Sure enough, it was old Miss Crosby (our other neighbour) out in her nighty and carpet slippers, trying to bury a copper kettle. She does it from time to time. She has developed a fear of nuclear war in her dotage, and seems to think she should conceal her savings in case she survives. I managed to persuade her, in a loud whisper, that she could leave it for a few hours more. Eventually she ambled back to the house, dragging the spade behind her. At the crack of dawn Nora Thorpe's feathered friend started screeching and woke me again. I yelled "Shut up" out of the window, and I think it went back into its hutch.

Now I'm having an early morning cup of tea in the kitchen. It's nice and quiet at last.

A Letter to Eric in Australia

5th April, 1992

Dear Eric,

I thought I'd write to you separately at work, to keep a separate line open, as it were. As you may know, I've already written to Maisie. It was very kind off you to have her for a few weeks. She has been worrying a bit about Alistair, and up to her neck in squabbles on the church council. A complete change should do her good. (It bloody well ought to, considering the cost of the flight.) She was greatly looking forward to it, and particularly seeing our common mother-in-law (!)

Actually, between you and me, we haven't got off to a very good start back at the ranch. The night after his mother left Alistair had a hell of a celebration disco in the loft, and cracked the ceiling of the main bedroom. 17 adults was obviously too much for the rafters. The surveyor warned us they weren't strong enough when we had it converted. Complaints from the vicar's wife, though I must say the noise was terrible. I had to stop it in the end.

Anyway, I'm hoping to get some serious writing done, now the house is blissfully quiet again. I've got some ideas out with publishers, and who knows, I may get something accepted. If there are problems your end, send me a note.

       Yours,

          William

William Tries another Publisher

10th April 1992

Dear Miss Boxer,

I was sorry to learn that your uncle is currently unavailable. I shall, however, send you the manuscript of the first volume of my autobiography, entitled '*A Swansea Boyhood*' under separate cover. Some might describe those years as uneventful, but the essence of literature lies (in <u>my</u> opinion) not so much in tinselly events as in sensitivity of expression.

In addition, I can propose a humorous novel, '*1770 Pacific Drive*', set in California, based on the activities of a mad psychoanalyst (outline enclosed). I am also working on a coffee-table book on the human foot. Perhaps you would be kind enough to forward this letter and the enclosures for you uncle's kind consideration in due course. Does he, incidentally, publish books of ornithological interest? If so, I could proffer a powerful idea which centres on an ecological disaster at a poultry farm in Kent.

May I add that I already enjoy an ongoing association with a prestigious publisher, but I have not yet signed any exclusive deal with him. I would be very happy to collaborate with Bristol Channel Publishers in addition.

Yours sincerely,

William Price.

P.S. Could you let me have some background information on your House, including lists of previous publications? I could not find the name in the local library, but the council has cut back so much, it's not true.

Mr. Boxer Writes a Nice Letter

13th April 1992

Dear Mr. Price,

My niece Doris told me just after I got back from me holiday break, that you wishes to publish through our House, with the good idea of attracting fame and making some money. And very good, too. I look forward to reading your outline '*1770 Pacific Drive*' which now lies on me desk, and to seeing your autobiography currently expected to arrive by second class post.

In reply to your question, I can say that the Bristol Channel Press is an entirely new venture, and if your book was accepted it would certainly be one of our first. I do, however, have considerable experience of publishing up until we closed my agency temporary last year, due, I should add, entirely to outside pressures and my wish to retire for a bit from commercial activities. We will now be publishing again.

B.C.P. is actively looking for good quality manuscripts, and I would like to encourage you to send us all that you have for our active appraisal. Please send everything on.

    Yours Sincerely,

        Henry Boxer, Chief Executive,
        Bristol Channel Press

1770 PACIFIC DRIVE (Publisher's Outline)

The hero and heroine are Seymour and Nancy Crust, both realtors, of 1770 Pacific Drive [fictitious names and addresses, of course]. They sleep in separate rooms because Nancy snores and Seymour has a malodorous form of foot-rot. Very early one morning Nancy, half awake, dreams that two naked and sexually aroused Zulu warriors have entered the bedroom and are endeavouring to penetrate her through her aural apertures, [ears], one on the right and one on the left. A moment later she wakes up in horror, only to hear someone scampering off. But she decides not to tell her husband, lest he considers it to be a suggestion for future nocturnal activity (he is rather inept in sexual matters, anyway). She becomes really worried when the dream is repeated, with the Zulus sporting floral garlands: all this regardless of the fact that she has always had simple, uncomplicated copulatory relations with her spouse.

(I think you will agree that this is a fine, intriguing start.)

Worried, she contacts her psychoanalyst, an elderly German consultant called Dr. Fritz Heidelberg. She has had occasional sittings with him for several years, as was fashionable in the Drive. On this occasion he listens with particular attention, but can only guarantee a complete cure if she takes a long and expensive course of treatment which he can devise for her. Despairing of finding the money, and convinced that her psychological state is almost hopeless, she decides to enter a Catholic convent and try a late vocation. She has noted that Seymour seems to be behaving ever more strangely, anyway.

What she does not know is that he has had three visions of Zulu warriors himself! At this point the plot appears to take a supernatural turn. The visions convince him that he is in fact going queer (although he had not noticed it before). He gets into touch with his psychoanalyst, who is also Dr. Heidelberg, though neither Seymour nor Nancy realise they have been sharing the same expertise. Dr. Heidelberg recommends a long and costly course of treatment with the prospect of certain success. Seymour, however, also decides he can't afford it, and on learning that Nancy has entered a convent decides to "come out of the closet". Since he was always rather athletic, he joins a gay weight-lifting club, and soon falls in love with a muscle-builder called Clint Faith.

The novel now seems to have reached, as it were, a symmetrical plateau, the main characters being propelled to their doom by sinister but unseen forces. At this point the scene shifts dramatically to a seedy diner in Oakland (across the bay from San Francisco) where two large Zimbabweans, both majoring in law at Berkeley University, are eating large portions of bacon and eggs. The door opens and who should shuffle in but Dr. Heidelberg, shabbily dressed so as not to attract attention. The reader senses that a partial denouement ["unknotting", French] is at hand, but only partial, because there are too many pages left over.

The conversation which ensues between the three reveals that the good doctor has come to pay them money. To put it briefly, the "nightmare" routine is something he has devised to boost the flagging demand for his psychiatric advice. It works like this: he gets copies of the keys his clients leave in the pockets of their coats in the waiting room (because he forbids metal objects on the couch). After elucidating the situation at selected clients' homes, keys are given to the Zimbabweans. The latter go along in the early hours of the morning, and having crept in and donned Zulu garb (or what there is of it) apply bursts of a mild amnesiac spray above the victims' pillows. When the latter are awakened by the visitors' activities, their confused state of mind and physical helplessness give them the impression that they are having a genuine nightmare. The negroes go off before the victims fully regain consciousness. The procedure is risky, but Dr. Heidelberg is desperate for clientèle.

The action of the novel next switches to a court-room, where a legal drama is being played out. Seymour has changed his name from Crust to Hope, and his former wife has become Sister Charity. She is suing him for half of the marital home which she wants to donate to the local Prostitutes for Peace Association (PPA). Seymour is contesting this because he requires the accommodation for a joint home with Clint. The case has attracted considerable attention in legal circles and among the public, and is known as the Faith, Hope and Charity Case.

Anyway, the final denouement involves some highly professional writing. Amongst the crowd in the courtroom sit, unwittingly, the two Zimbabweans (sent unwittingly by their law tutor), Dr. Heidelberg (in dark glasses, so as not to be recognised), and several members of the PPA. When Sister Charity is called to the witness box she catches sight of the erstwhile Zulus and faints. Ambulance men take her to a local infirmary, amid much wailing from Peace girls. Seymour then also recognises the pair, and realises that they are somehow involved in his unfortunate lurch into gaydom. He attempts to accost them, starts a fight, and is hauled away to jail by the police. His friend Clint has hysterics and has to be led to the quiet room. Finally the two negroes recognise Dr. Heidelberg and try to attack him, because he owes them money for several dream appearances. The court room lapses into pandemonium.

The final scene: Dr. Heidelberg, his professional practice now finally in ruins, decides to throw it all in and become a Rabbi. He is last observed walking towards an Oakland synagogue with a prayer shawl over his shoulders.

The End.

Mr. Boxer Writes an Interesting Letter

23rd April, 1992

Dear Mr. Price,

This is a brief letter to let you know that I and my professional readers have gone through your manuscript '*A Swansea Boyhood*', word by word, and we all got a big kick out of it, (honest). The language is nice and clear, no hard words that might turn folk off, and one can almost hear the lilt of a nice Welsh accent. You included a lot of funny bits – we all enjoyed the hilairius passages about catshit in the coal-house, the mess the window-cleaner with one leg got himself in when the sash gave way, and the accidental drowning at the baptismal service in Caersalem. We was all in fits.

Wecan then gladly turn our attention to '*1770 Pacific Drive*' which, to judge from the few pages I have read, bulges with literary promise.

Our response is that we would like to go forward firmly with '*Boyhood*', and aim for vigorus world-wide sales. We shall, however, need to consider certain technical questions, like wheres the money coming from to start off with. Also we would have to have from you an absolute undertaking that no other publishers are in on the game. Respectable publishers like Bristol Channel don't like tusselling over the rights of really good books like this one is.

We look forward to hearing from you, particularly about the money.

    Yours sincerely,

    Henry Boxer, Principal
    Bristol Channel Press

DIARY – *William Gets Good News*

24rd April, 1992

Got home from work to find glorious news awaiting me – letter of acceptance from Bristol Channel Press. Absolutely over the moon. Alistair was out, so I did an unassuming poached egg on toast for supper.

The evening was nice and I took a deckchair out into the garden to have a quiet gin and tonic with myself. I have found that beverage to be very inspirational, given the right surroundings. Of course, that is the sort of thing I can only do when Maisie is not messing about in the bloody flowerbed. Why are women so fussy? Confucius believed they had smaller brains.

I settled back to foretaste the joys of publication, and speculate a little on my forthcoming life in print. A full-throated thrush chortled in the lilac. The daisies which bespatter our rear lawn had not yet quite closed their tired yellow eyes, and still gazed lovingly at the heavens. I noted that the smell of spilt engine oil had lessened perceptibly.

'*A Swansea Boyhood*'... It did indeed have a promising, even noble ring. The excitement of proof-correcting. Seeing the first bound copy. The telephone calls from the local papers to arrange personal interviews. They would no doubt insist on giving me a full page in the centre fold, with an appropriate announcement on page one. The invitations to talk at choice local venues, – not least the freemasons' monthly function and the university. The reviews in the better national newspapers. Substantial royalty cheques. The discussion on the BBC book programmes. The eagerly awaited second book – which would probably be '*1770 Pacific Drive*',... "a storyline of startling originality, delicately erotic without vulgarity..."

I was just considering the content of my letter of resignation to that old bugger Whitby, when a terrible screech interrupted my reverie, and almost caused me to spill the contents of my glass – or those which remained. Nora Thorpe had started to feed their peacock next door. At that moment my eye fell on Pinkey, who was sitting on the crazy paving, evidently trying to catch a few of her fleas. I must confess that after Maisie's departure I had forgotten to continue the treatment, necessitated, Maisie claimed, by intimate furry contact with the vicarage Tom. In the twinkling of an eye I had grasped the hapless beast and stuffed her through a convenient hole in the hedge. I think that did the trick: in any case, the delicious silence which followed was broken only momentarily by the bang of the door of the bird's hutch, as it was (I imagine) precipitously closed.

I have solved, it would appear, two of my life's most pressing problems – publication of my prose, and the suppression of an unpleasant, jarring noise. With those thoughts in my mind I retired happily to bed, where I am writing these lines.

Another Letter to Penarth

26th April 1992

Dear Mr. Boxer,

I was most gratified by the receipt of your letter of the 23rd April with your astute comments on my autobiography. It is obvious to me that you and your colleagues have read my text with great care. Such an evaluation from a man of letters is most flattering. At the same time I can assure you that there is plenty more where that came from. Apart from the manuscripts I now have in hand, you may in due course like to see an older novel, on my shelf for some years, entitled "Leagues Apart", an incisive tale of dissension between two American baseball teams. (I have always been interested in the USA).

May I confirm that my autobiography is solely with you, and will go nowhere else. It was shown to one House only, which did not rise to the occasion. I would be very happy to commit publication to you alone. One thing more: it is usual to call on the services of a solicitor for contractual matters, and I would suggest the gentleman who occasionally acts for us at Whitby's, when customers don't pay.

I look forward to hearing about the next steps. It's all very exciting.

       Yours sincerely,

          William Price

Maisie Worries a Little

1ˢᵗ May 1992

Dear William,

Thank you for your telephone call yesterday. I'm glad you got around to it at last. After all, I've been here for weeks, and all I've had was the one call on the day after I arrived. And the one letter. I suppose I was expected to believe that no news is good news. But William, if you really want to become a writer, I suggest you start by WRITING TO YOUR WIFE. You know how I worry. And all that distance from home. I can understand Alistair, he's young and thoughtless. It was up to you to get him to send me a few words, as he promised. It's your fault. After the first week, Mummy actually said it was strange you hadn't written, Daddy was never like that, for all his faults. She's a kindly soul, you're most unfair to her. I didn't like to ring myself, because of the telephone bills, Eric is a bit tight that way. Please try not to let it go so long again. And where was Alistair when you phoned? If he's found any new girl friends, I hope you encourage him to bring them home, to see who it is.

Conny and Eric are lucky, with their boy safely into architecture. I hope, incidentally, you're not seeing too much of that dreadful Charlie French.

Well, I don't suppose you two worry much about me, but I can tell you I get a bit terrified at times, on account of the eucalyptus forest next door. Eric said it gives off fumes, all you have to do is strike a match, and the whole thing can literally explode. I didn't think his joke about roast kangaroo was the least bit funny. And to tell you the truth I've hardly slept since. I keep listening for the flames crackling. A couple of days ago I nearly got bitten by a poisonous lizard with a blue mouth. It was horrible.

The sun is a bit too much for the garden, though I haven't said anything. It wouldn't suit us at Acacia. I hope you are keeping things nice and tidy. Please give Nora my regards, and tell her Conny takes me to the church services in Brisbane. And be nice to Miss Crosby, the dear old thing.

When you next write please send the pictures you took of Alistair making sandcastles at Southend when he was small, Mummy never saw them. Also, see that Mrs. Wrangle does the kitchen stove as well as the floors, she'll give it a miss if she thinks you are not looking. And especially the toilet. Above all, think of promotion at Wilkinson's, and consider the neighbours and don't waste time on those silly manuscripts. That's all for now.

Love,   Maisie.

DIARY – *Trouble at the Shop*

5th May 1992

Another sale lost in the shop.

Shortly after Ben and I had finished lunch in the back office Mr. Whitby called me out to the floor. With him was a very fat, untidily-dressed man with long hair and a pronounced squint.

"I wonder whether you could help this gentleman", said the manager with his Grade Two customer intonation. "He requires some glass-fronted cabinets, and I think we have just the thing. The Aldergrove Home Display Units, in the mahogany veneer, may well be what he wants."

"Do come this way, sir," I said, with the hint of ingratiation I had perfected for Grade Twos. A friendly gleam twinkled in my eye.

"Here they are. As you can see, they are nicely leaded with genuine mock-Tudor glass, and designed to show off any china tea service to the very best advantage."

"Tea service?" said the gent. "Who said anything about a tea service? No time for bloody nonsense like that."

"Most of our customers" I said, "purchase these items with china in view, but of course, *à chacun son gout*, as the French say. They are well finished, but they only cost £199.95 each. The cabinets, I mean, not the French. A-hm."

He gave me a curious look and leaned over to inspect one, disappearing, as it were, behind his own elephantine posterior. I wondered whether his squint made it easier to peer into corners.

"Actually, this looks alright. I need them for my reference materials."

"Excellent for the purpose. As a matter of fact, my wife objects to open bookshelves, because they gather dust. I use one of these myself. To keep my collections of Kipling and Bernard Shaw."

The customer looked startled.

"Kipling?" he said, incredulously. "Bernard Shaw? Do anyone read them any more?"

I could not restrain myself:

> "Take up the white man's burden,
> Send for the best ye breed –
> Go bind your sons to exile
> To serve your captives' need;
> To wait in heavy harness
> On fluttered folk and wild –
> Your new-caught, sullen peoples,
> Half devil and half child."

"Racist, elitist rubbish. Ought to be bloody well banned."

"A fine, ringing stanza".

"What the fuck is 'fluttered', anyway?"

"I don't know. But the occasional word doesn't matter. It's the overall effect."

"Well, we won't have any of that at the poly."

"Would you like to hear another? This country has gone a long way down the path of censorship, but thank God I can still read Kipling at my own hearth, if I want to. Or anyone else. I also happen to enjoy Dickens.

"Jesus", exclaimed the customer, his squint assuming (or so it seemed) an even worse angle. "You can't have read Peter Ackroyd's biography. Dickens' political views were gruesome."

He began to breath heavily.

"The quality of literature is not necessarily a function of the author's political views, or life-style, for that matter. Look at Marlowe, who got himself murdered, or Oscar Wilde."

"Perhaps I should tell you" the gentleman retorted ponderously, "that I lecture in a Department of Contemporary English, and I know a thing or two about literature. We chucked all of that balderdash out of the curriculum years ago. I am proud to say I played a leading part in the campaign. Personally, I stopped reading Kipling and Dickens when I was fourteen. Anyway, they're being proved worthless by our new Weighted Criticism project."

"Weighted Criticism?"

"It's creating a sensation. I thought every writer knew about it. We are building up an idea matrix of about four hundred conceptual clusters, each weighted on a five-point positive to negative scale. A group of inputters is going through selected texts (the so-called classical English novels) page by page, punching the main clusters into a central data bank. We've written a programme, with close approximative weightings, to classify the clusters. The computer patterns are then compared with the sort of pattern a work of literature of that kind *should* have in an egalitarian, emancipated, multi-racial society. The divergences so far are incredible. That's what I want the cabinets for, actually. The tapes. They're very bulky."

"I would have thought some steel shelving from the army surplus store…"

"I beg your pardon", said the gent, with a sudden iciness in his voice, "we are talking about my professional literary activities. And about my living room. How would *you* like to look at a set of bloody steel shelves all the evening?…

"Well, er…"

"I don't think that Wilkinson's will be able to help with this item," he said firmly. "The cabinets look a bit… outmoded, anyway. Good day."

And, like my sales commission, he disappeared from sight.

A Really Nice Publisher

8th May, 1992

Dear Mr. Price,

Thank you for having our valuabel services, and we are sure you will not be disappointed with us. Publishers like us are always delited when they can make talented writers happy, quite apart from the money in it, which we can discuss again later. To reply to what you wrote about solicitors: our House has of course had some of them, but we never call them in for simple matters like this. Apart from their bills, which can be sky high, they may cause distrust which, I hope will never get into our day-to-day working relations.

We are preparing our usual Publisher's Agreement which we are sure will suit your reqwirements. One thing did, however, occur to me. Next week my colleague Mr. Joshua Phipps and I have other clients to see around the Metropolis. Also, my niece, who spoke to you on the phone, has just finished her A-Levels and has been called to attend for an ordition in a West End Theatre. She wants to be an actress. We shall be fairly flexible about transport since we can all drive up in the company Mercedes. So I wonder whether you would be available for a meeting – possibly even at your home while we are up there. If so we would like to have the opportunity to meet you and your Lady wife in comfortable surroundings, and you could sign the agreement on the spot.

In any case we look forward to seeing you, and please confirm.

    Yours Sincerely,

    Henry Boxer, Principal

William Makes Arrangements

11th May, 1992

Dear Mr. Boxer,

May I acknowledge, with a pleasure no doubt equaling your own, receipt of your letter of the 8th May. I was delighted to learn that you are coming to London, and look forward to seeing you for substantive discussions on the spot. I shall arrange especially to take some time off from the sales floor for that purpose. No doubt you will have some samples of your publications to show me – printed pages, cover designs, dust jackets, etc., if not from your newly established House, then from past ones. I think scrolled corners, if economic, are particularly attractive. Do you anticipate any graphic work? I have a number of old photographs which would lend local colour, and might well improve sales potential. We must also consider publishing dates: one close to my Wife's birthday would be most apposite. Sadly, I have to tell you that my Wife is currently enjoying the delights of rural Australia, so cannot be present. But I hope there will be other opportunities for a meeting.

I think it would be nice if we indeed had a publisher's lunch together, so I shall expect you at our residence, unless I hear otherwise, about one o'clock. Your chauffeur is no doubt experienced in finding his way around, but in any case I enclose a small sketch map to facilitate location. The best landmarks are the spire of St. Mary's the Virgin and the chemist's shop on the corner.

Hasta, as they say in Spain, la vista.

Yours sincerely,

William Price.

Note to Alistair

14th May 1992

8 am.

Dear Alistair,

Another quick note before I go off to work. What time did you get in last night, for God's sake?

Anyway, can you AT LAST do something about the pool of motor cycle oil on your mother's crazy paving, before it sinks in? She'll go beserk if it's stained when she gets back (which it might be). Some guests are supposed to be coming to see me and they may go out into the garden. What's wrong with working in the garage? You could move the car. Try white spirit, Vim, and a bit of elbow grease. You can't expect Mrs. Wrangle to do that sort of thing. she grumbles enough as it is.

Also, a letter from the bank manager happened to fall from your jacket pocket when I was hanging it up last night. You never said anything to <u>me</u> about an overdraft. That's the motorbike, I suppose. We must have a talk when our paths next meet. This evening?

Dad.

DIARY – *The Publisher's Lunch*

20th May 1992

Mr Boxer and co. arrived today as planned, or rather not quite as planned, since the company Mercedes was being serviced, and they had to come by train and the no. 83 bus. Their visit was a little overshadowed by the presence of Jack Marples and his mate, who came to do the ceiling. I had not anticipated so unfortunate a clash, especially as the mate sang incessantly as he laboured. However, it had to be tolerated.

I must say I was curious to meet Mr. Boxer, my potential benefactor. He looked rather like a middle-aged city-gent, a little obese and balding, with a moustache and slight cockney accent, But a nice combination, I thought, of literary sensitivity and business acumen. He came with young Mr. Phipps, his junior in the firm, and his niece Doris. Mr. Phipps recalled the kind of person who goes to greyhound races, and was on occasions a little irreverent. The young lady was definitely what one would (in my youth) have called tarty. She appeared to be in her mid-twenties, and was physically well, if not over-developed, with excessive use of make-up. I was dismayed to note that Alistair took an immediate liking to her. She confirmed that she intended to go on the stage, and had come up with her uncle to be auditioned for Orphelia in the West End. I must say I had never envisaged Hamlet's girlfriend in such an embodiment.

Before we sat down to lunch our guests expressed an interest in seeing the house (which, as Mr. Boxer noted) was very professionally furnished. He commented on a number of our small objects of art, including Maisie's watercolours from Minehead. The meal itself went very well indeed. I gave them some nice salad with a tin of

West's pink salmon and a bottle of wine, followed by some semolina pudding I had prepared the night before. With raspberry jam. We used Maisie's best china and cutlery. Everyone tucked in with great relish.

"A very nice lunch, if I may say so", declared Mr. Boxer as we came to the end. "The salmon was particularly succulent."

"A hell of a sight nicer than you've been getting recently, anyways," said Mr. Phipps, with a grin.

"Uncle Henry knows how to rough it, when need be", Doris added, slyly.

Mr. Boxer, I could see, was a little annoyed. I looked at him with some puzzlement.

"You have, I gather, been away from home" I said, helpfully. "Did not the little girl who answered the telephone say that you were bird-watching?"

Mr. Phipps nearly choked with laughter.

"That", said Mr. Boxer, after an uneasy pause, " was Doris's little daughter. I wonder what she told you? She fantasises a great deal! I have in fact spent some months visiting writers doing time in Her Majesty's Prisons. It is something my firm will be specialising in. After reading a number of amazing descriptions of prison life in the popular press I realised that doing a stretch can bring out people's extrordinary literary talent, that they didn't even know they had. So I went off looking for it in the right places. My aim (though I say it myself) was not so much going after the money, but giving them a helping hand what they deserved. And some of them had a real rough time in there. One gentleman, for example, who got hisself done for GBH…"

"GBH?"

"Grievous bodily harm – was writing a nice little novel about a poor orphan girl with one leg who got caught up pushing dope. The action was set in the backstreets of Brixton, as he remembered them before he got done in 1985. He had hoped that the Governor would parole him, so that he could refresh his memory and add some colourful touches to his prose. Buy the Governor was a hard man, and refused everything he asked him for. Apart from that, the screws was green with envy…"

"The screws?…"

"The prison warders, who gave him hell, poor sod. They kept on stealing his pencils and crumpling his manuscripts up."

"My God".

"My dear Mr. Price (may I finish off the wine?) that's just one of many cases I knows of. What about the young poet who was imprisoned just for enquiring about some poor boy's health outside a public toilet? My unfortunate friend's offer of food and shelter was maliciously misconstrued by a copper in plain clothes, who done him in a flash. He is now using his years inside to write odes about Greek boys' physiques. That was obviously, someone whose pen could benefit from being helped a bit. We must see whether we can get any of his stuff published by the time he gets outside. He'll certainly need the money."

"We can all use some of that, can't we, ducky?" said Miss Boxer, with a wink. I think she was getting a little tipsy.

"Perhaps", said Mr. Boxer, "having finished our repast, this is an apt moment to turn to contractual matters. Mr.

Phipps, do you have the Publisher's Agreement in your pocket? Mr. Price would no doubt like to look over it before signing. Though I am sure there is not much to add."

The junior fumbled for a moment in his worn brief case and pulled out a closely typed sheet, which he presented to me with a florid gesture.

"Here it is!"

A glow of pleasure passed through me. The partners watched me closely, no doubt enjoying my clearly positive reactions. Then Mr. Boxer quickly handed me a pen. A glance at the content had indeed assured me that this was the document I had been long waiting for, and I signed on the spot.

That was, in effect, the climax of the visit. Mr. Boxer, looking at his watch, declared that it was getting late, and they should really be off, if Doris were to get to her audition in time. We all walked to the bus stop together.

A splendid start to my writing career.

William Writes to Maisie

22nd May, 1992

Dear Maisie,

I have not written to you before because I have been waiting for a bit of good news! And now it has come! A big I TOLD YOU SO!

I have just managed to hook a genuine publisher for my autobiography, a nice little firm in Penarth. Yesterday, the Principal – a chap called Mr. Boxer – came to lunch at our house with his clerk and niece. I got the best china out, and it all went back with nothing broken! I think you would have liked Mr. Boxer (perhaps you'll meet him later), he's a nice cultured man in his early fifties, balding, with his remaining hair carefully combed down, in a pin-striped suit and gold-rimmed spectacles. He also had a signet ring on his little right finger, always a mark of discernment, I think. You remember I wanted to wear one in the shop, but Mr. Whitby said it looked sissy. That's the sort of place I work in. Anyway, Mr. Boxer made a reference to Ovid, the ancient Greek poet, and is apparently a leading figure in the Prison Reform movement. I signed their agreement straight away: they'll probably be taking a novel from me as well. The '*Boyhood*' book will be brought out at a commercially propitious moment, finely printed and well bound, with several tasteful drawings and photographs. Mr. Boxer expects five thousand copies to sell out in South Wales alone!

Well, there it is. I'll keep you posted. Everything in the house is fine, and Mrs. Wrangle DID do the stove. Drop us a line soon, Alistair looks forward to your letters.

Love, William

... And to Eric

22ⁿᵈ May, 1992

Dear Eric,

All sorts of exciting things happening here! I thought I'd write to tell you, I'd like to have your opinion, you were in journalism once. I'm writing to Maisie by the same post, but for you – a few extra details!

I've just had a real stroke of luck. I've hooked a publisher for my autobiography, a firm in Penarth. Yesterday the Principal (a chap called Boxer) came to lunch with his clerk and niece. He produced a very favourable impression on me: in his early fifties, balding (with the strands stuck down), pin-stripe suit and gold-rimmed spectacles. A signet ring on his little finger, for style. He's obviously very knowledgeable about literary matters. He made a few references to Shakespeare, and is apparently a leading figure in the prison reform movement.

I signed his standard agreement, and he assured me I am getting a very good deal. He accepts the manuscript as it is, and will bring it out as he says, at a propitious moment, finely printed and well bound, with artistic drawings and photographs. Ten thousand copies to start with, most of which should sell out in a few days. He does not recommend a larger print-run, preferring to err on the side of caution. I get the usual royalty of five per cent after one hundred thousand copies.

I got a special deal on the Publisher's Advance. I have now gone through the document carefully and learn that Bristol Channel Press require only £3,000 to get started (which Boxer says is way below the going rate) plus a share of the printing and binding costs (£1,000). They seem to have no doubt that the book will earn several times that amount in the first year. I have a whole month to get the money. It'll have to be an overdraft, I suppose.

Well, that's the picture, not bad, is it? Let me know what you think. Hope all goes well with you.

Regards, William.

A Word of Advice

25th May, 1992

Dear William,

(I hope you don't mind first names among friends!). May I begin by thanking you for the really tastey lunch which you done for Doris, Joshua and me, the Cyprus wine was really nice. I hope there will be more meetings like that as your writing progresses. On another positive note I would like to tell you that everyone in the office have now had time to look through your '*1770 Pacific Drive*', and think that this could also be a fantastic block-buster, with the prose of your normal quality.

In any case we want to encourage you to go forward, so when we get the manuscript we could offer you the same sort of terms you got already. We expect to hear from you about the money you owe us a.s.p., so we can get the whole thing rolling.

       Yours sincerely,

        Henry

Part II

A Police Report

29th May 1992

From Police Sergeant Woman Copplestone.

<u>REPORTED THEFT</u>

I proceeded to No 17, Acacia Crescent at 11am as arranged to take a statement from the owner, Mr. William Price, on the reported theft of certain household effects for insurance purposes.

The informant stated that family heirlooms, namely, a set of 12 Queen Anne silver spoons he valued at £2,000 and a Georgian tea pot, valued at £1,000, had disappeared from an unlocked display cabinet in the sitting room. Their absence was first noted yesterday. There seems to be no doubt about their disappearance, dust marks on the shelf indicating the former presence of square and round-based objects. There were no signs of breaking or entering. Mr. Price normally lives on the premises with his son Alistair. The known visitors during the day were Mrs. Ada Wrangle , the cleaner, three representatives of a publishing firm in South Wales (Mr. Henry Boxer, Miss Doris Boxer, Mr. Joshua Phipps, and two decorators, Mr. Jack Matlock and his mate Mr. Derek Ulman).

Mr. Price is convinced of the honesty of all of these people, and does not want police intrusion which might offend. The informant has the unfortunate habit of leaving the doors unlocked when he is working in the garden or goes out, and this happened on the day in question, when he accompanied his guests to the bus stop and did some shopping. If a sneak thief had entered the premises it is doubtful whether the workmen would have been aware of it, as they were upstairs. Mr. Price's son also left the house.

I warned Mr. Price to be much more careful in future and suggested he join the local Neighbourhood Watch. He said this would undoubtedly appeal to his lady wife when she returns from Australia later this summer.

<u>Action</u>: Register loss.

A Letter from Sunrise Assurance, Ltd

1st June, 199.

Dear Mr. Price,

We are in receipt of your letter regarding the apparent theft of heirlooms to the estimated valued of £3,000 as reported to the police. We cannot, however, send you the normal claim form as following your instructions of the 3rd January of this year your household policy was not renewed. You referred in your letter to the relative security of your possessions and cost of our policy. We normally urge circumspection on our customers, and regret that this has happened.

Please contact us if you wish to avail yourself of our services in future. May we assure you that our rates remain extremely competitive.

Yours sincerely,

David Mayfield,
Insurance Advisor

... And the Coop Bank

2nd *June, 1992*

Dear Mr. Price,

Thank you for your letter of the 26th instant regarding an increase in your current overdraft or other possible financial arrangement. As was explained to you over the telephone, we view you and your Lady Wife as valued customers of long standing and look forward to serving the needs of your family in the future. Our various services are described in a number of very readable leaflets.

In line with our customer relations policy we shall not be pressing you for an early repayment of your existing overdraft, though we would request you not to fall any further behind. I cannot comment on the financial affairs of other members of your family, but when considering loan requests we have to take the whole picture of debts, apart from your own, into consideration. Your son recently indicated to us that he needed a loan to buy a motorcycle. I would be happy to look at the whole situation when there is a marked change for the better, as in the circumstances we certainly could not consider any further advances. I enjoyed our last meeting but feel that another would be a little superfluous at present.

    Yours sincerely,

        Arthur Saunders
        (Assistant Manager)

DIARY – *The Big Sales Day*

6th June, 1992

The last few hours have again convinced me, if any convincing were needed, that purveying household furniture is not what God created me for. Sometimes I compare my state to that of Anthony Trollope, who spent years as a miserable post office clerk, though I am not certain I can match his talent.

There is no doubt that Wilkinson's BIG SALE days palpably shorten the life of the staff at the Teckley branch, as it goads them to greater effort in the hope of being a bit richer by five o'clock. Things started badly yesterday evening, when old Whitby asked me to get some sale notices, of which he keeps a large selection, stuck up in the window. I had made what I thought was rather a good job of it, with an orange-coloured "Everything Must Go" circle, surrounded by white angels' wings with "Reductions", "Sale", etcetera, when he rushed into the window area, shouting that we were not selling sunflowers or fried eggs. The "Everything Must Go" poster particularly irritated him: although that might be the desired outcome, he said, Wilkinson's always avoided vulgarity, and this was no sell-out. Respectable customers might be discouraged. I was obliged to scrape it all off with a dessert knife and a bowl of soapy water, though it was not easy, and attracted the attention of a number of gawping children going home from school.

This morning the first customer did not appear until a disappointing twenty past ten, by which time both Miss Kingsley and young Ben were distinctly nervous. Miss Kingsley had put on the ghastly floral frock she uses for the Christmas party, and had her hair permed. Ben looked as nondescript as usual. However, I passed the time planning "The Foot in History" behind our Kitchen Furniture section. By lunchtime things had picked up: Ben actually managed to shift two Sundowner settees and Miss Kingsley sold a dining suite.

Things turned bad again in the afternoon, when Mrs. Alfreda Topley came into the shop. Mr. Whitby had, in fact, informed me that she might try for a bargain. Her husband was Grand Master of the Teckley Freemason's Lodge, which might soon need refurnishing, and she has connections with Larehall's, the local printers and publishers, who could offer some cheap advertising. She was therefore definitely a *persona grata*. As soon as he saw her formidable black-clad figure crossing the threshold Mr. Whitby glowed with his Grade One Customer oldy-worldy charm. I thought for a moment that he was even going to kiss her hand, but he couldn't quite bring himself to do it.

"Mrs. Topley", he intoned, "How delightful to see you!... How is your husband? We were in the Army Catering Corps together, you know... The fireside chairs you bought from us added, I hope, an extra miggin of comfort to your lovely home? Quite satisfactory, was they? Can we be of any help today? We have some nice bargains on the floor!"

"I'm sure you have, Mr. Whitby", said she, graciously. "In fact my niece is getting married in a couple of weeks, and I thought perhaps a small side-table or bookcase, not too expensive, of course..." Mr. Whitby turned meaningfully to his immediate subordinate, (me), who was standing behind them. "Mr. Price (he said) no doubt can help us. Price, do we still have that nice antique-style hall table, or did it go to Lady Watkin's? Ah, yes, there it is, over there..." We were about to proceed to closer inspection when Ben came to say that Head Office wanted to speak to him on the telephone. As far as I was concerned, the opportunity was not to be missed.

"I gather, Mrs. Topley", I said, as soon as he turned his back, "that you have contacts with Larehall's Publishers". Mrs. Topley seemed a little surprised by my interest. "My husband is a director of the firm, and has been almost since it started. Do you have any publishing interests yourself? I would have thought selling furniture in today's world is work enough as it is."

"As a matter of fact, Mrs. Topley, I spend only eight hours a day in Wilkinson's, most of my remaining time being devoted to literary pursuits. I do indeed have a corpus of prose which I would like to see in print."

"It is my opinion, Mr. Price, that one should choose a path in life as soon as one is mature, and stick to it throughout. A secure job in a furnishing shop on Teckley High Street would be the dream of many. My husband tells me that authorship is chancy, and most of what is written is balderdash. He has always stuck to the business side of things himself." She paused. "A mixture of styles is always, I think, to be regretted."

"Whenever I write anything I try and be consistent. My autobiography, for example, rings quite differently from my fictional prose."

"I was referring to your side-table. Its Regency-style legs hardly match the mock Venetian mosaic on top. It's the sort of thing you might find in a cheap ice-cream parlour. I wonder who ordered it? Now *this* table looks a little more promising, how much does it cost? Can you see the label? It's tied underneath."

I had just got down on my knees to try and catch the damn thing, which was hanging underneath, when my nostrils caught the odour of curry and chips, foul indeed at four o'clock in the afternoon. A pair of ragged, bejeaned calves came into sight, accompanied by the uncovered lower limbs of a young female. The owners had the impertinence to settle themselves in the remaining Sundowner. Alistair's voice rang through the shop, backed by a female giggle.

"Hello Dad! On our hands and knees again, are we? More capitalist enterprise? Or just trying to get a better view of the lady's knees? Ha, ha, ha."

I struggled to my feet to find my offspring and (to my astonishment) Miss Doris Boxer, both comfortably ensconced and grinning hugely. "For God's sake get off that settee! You'll get curry on the arms!"

"I brought Doris in to have a look at the shop", Alistair explained, "and have a sit-down lunch. She's my new girl-friend." Doris added a broad wink. I noted earlier that she was good at it.

"Alistair, this is *not* the place to eat curry and chips in," I hissed. "For Christ's sake get out! It smells terrible."

Mrs. Topley had moved back a step or two. "I think, Mr. Price," she said, with a scarcely perceptible sniff, "I have seen all I need to for the moment. I don't think Wilkinson's have what I want."

That was the moment Whitby chose to get back from the phone. Disaster was all too apparent, and as was his pained expression.

"Get those kids out of here quick" he snapped, "or I'll throw them out meself. ... Nothing suitable here, Mrs.

Topley? No…? We do have a number of interesting items on the upper floor. They are not reduced, but represent very good value."

"Thank you, Mr. Whitby, I think I have seen, and indeed smelt, all I wish to in your shop for the time being. I have one or two other places to visit, anyway. Do you often accommodate diners?."

And with that Mrs. Alfreda Topley stalked out.

Whitby's further comment will find no place in these pages, it is too tedious to consider. The incident may have given Alistair and his girlfriend a laugh, but did nothing to improve my prospects at Wilkinson's. I'll bloody well tell them so, too, when I see them. I wonder if Doris got that acting job?

The Publisher's Advance

10th June, 1992

Dear William,

We have now got our nose to the grindstone planning the page layout of *'A Swansea Boyhood'* and also doing the picture stuff. Would you please let us know if you would like to have this fine volume dedicated to someone, like a full page at the beginning. You might like to have the dedication nicely boxed, which would cost a bit extra.

Under the terms of the Publisher's Agreement, as you no doubt noted, half of the Publisher's Advance was due on signature. Obviously we have been flexible so far, but time passes don't it, and we would be grateful to have your check for one thousand grand and five hundred by first class post.

We are still looking for good authors like you are, and would like to know about any of your author friends whose stuff will sell. You may be interested to know that our House has started an Imprisoned Writers Benefit Fund, for which donations are always welcome.

We look forward to hearing from you very soon.

    Yours sincerely,

    Henry Boxer

Letter to Carmarthen Caravans, Ltd.

13th June, 1992

Dear Mr. Seldon,

As you know, we have a fine caravan at your park in Carmarthen. My wife and I have fitted it out beautifully (Worcester carpet, chintz curtains and loose covers on the furniture). I am in need of some cash and would like to put it on sale. Please let me know whether you would be interested in handling the transaction. How much do you think the caravan would be worth, with the parking site included? Would you please also let me know your terms.

I look forward to hearing from you as soon as convenient.

Yours sincerely,

William Price

Maisie Reassured

15th June 1992

Dear Maisie,

It was lovely to hear your voice again, despite the eerie other-world echo. Pity the calls aren't cheaper.

It was nice to have your congratulations about my literary success, though I must say I detected a hint of scepticism. Family approbation can be important to an author at times, especially while pursuing an arduous commercial career! I wonder how my dear mother in law reacted to the good news.

The people from the Bristol Channel Press hope to produce a very attractive volume by the end of the year, though the actual publishing date will be entirely at their discretion. Wouldn't it be marvellous if they got it out in time for your birthday? They have asked me to think about a nice dedication, to yourself of course. And possibly Alistair. Let me know what you would like to have.

Now with regard to the things you asked me about:

1. The borders are watered regularly and the lawn is doing fine.

2. The typed envelope was in fact from Torrington Old Girls Association. You are invited to the next annual get-together, and they're asking you to sing a soulful ballad again.

3. Everything at home (including A.) is fine. The cleaners sent all the curtains back and they are paid for. Mrs. Wrangle is still coming in to do the floors.

4. Various folk, like Fred and Annie, and Charlie French, have rung up to ask how you are, best regards, etc.

If anything unexpected crops up just give me a <u>one minute</u> telephone call. Otherwise just write.

Look after yourself. We think about you often.

    Love,

       W.

P.S. Incidentally, Auntie Martha's Queen Anne spoons and tea pot seem to have got mislaid. You didn't take them to Australia, did you? I mean, as a gift, without telling me?

P.P.S. I think the cat's pregnant again, probably by Miss Crosby's Tom. We will really have to have her done when you get back. Miss Crosby is still trying to bury things, poor dear.

P.P.P.S. Everything fine here, Mum! Keep it cool. A.

Alistair's Billet Doux

16th June, 1992

Dear Do,

Theres a disco at the poly tomorrow in aid of Somalia but the tickets only cost two quid and I hope you can come with me. I got the tickets anyway. Since you came into my life things have been totally different as I have never been in love before, really, dont take any notice of what my friends said yesterday about Suggy, they'll say anything for a laugh. At last I know what it means to have a really close person to share everthing with. I get a charge when I just look into them eyes of yours.

It isnt easy being the only child and living with your parents who are square and church-going with it, for instance they kept me in the choir till my voice broke and I put my foot down. Sometimes I wonder why they havent toped themselves from the boredom, its wicked, but they seem to go on and on. Everyones the same I suppose when they get middle aged and let yourself go. Mind, Dad is all right, as long as you dont take too much notice of him. Hes all into Wilkinsons furniture and writting novels. Anyway, I hope your new job is OK, are you really on the stage? When can I come and see you? I expect its terrific. If you get more trouble with your landlady you can come an stay with us, theres room upstairs. Can you cook? I think we should see more of one another anyway!! last time was the greatest.

Love and I mean it, Alistair.

DIARY – *Night thoughts*

19th June 1992

I hold that one of the tasks of a good diarist is to recount interesting, nay, lively incident, and lay before the reader a plethora of agreeable anecdote. Gloomy thoughts and nightmare should find but little space on his pages, most reader's lives being dismal enough already. That is, unless he is a Dostoyevski or Koestler, which I am probably not. Yet I must spare a moment for the darker thoughts which have just recently burdened my consciousness.

I awoke in the dead of night after a dream in which I surprised Mr. Boxer in his office having an amorous telephone conversation with Maisie. Somehow I knew it was she at the other end of the line. On seeing me Mr. Boxer replaced the receiver, took our Publishing Agreement out of his drawer, and deliberately tore it up. Next I found myself opening a letter from Maisie' solicitors, demanding £4,092 for the lost silverware. Then she, Mr. Boxer, Alistair and Doris Boxer drove past in open tourer, singing and towing our caravan down to Barry. It was grotesque.

I lay awake for some time, pondering my plight. The very basketwork of my existence is being stretched to breaking point by the financial strains of publication. Was I to fail, and my talent ever remain buried under a bushel in Acacia Avenue, for the lack of a few thousand pounds? Was there nothing I could sell to obtain this paltry sum? The miseries of my daily life filtered before my sleepless eyes. Doing the garden, with Maisie looking on. Trying to house-train Alistair. His motor-bike. Cleaning bits of Georgian silver. Showing customers how to open the Sundowner folding bed. Drinking Miss Kingley's powdered coffee. Listening to Fred Thorpe's terrible sermons. Would life be ever thus? Could I find a solution to my multiple predicaments, and gain a modest place in the ranks of contemporary authors?

My heart pounded ever louder in my breast as my emotions intensified. I began to listen to it intently. Perhaps a heart-attack was imminent? In a moment or two I became aware that it was *not* in fact my heart, but a regular thumping sound coming through the ceiling from Alistair's bedroom. Since deep sleep is one of his specialities, and this involves lying inert for hours on end, I was puzzled. What was he up to? A snatch of female laughter provided the answer.

I suspect it's that Doris. I must have a word with him tomorrow to put a bloody stop to it. After all, there are limits. I never ever seem to be able to catch him, he's always out. Things are getting completely out of control.

Another Note to Alistair

20th June, 1992

Dear Alistair,

Just a quick note before I go off to work. It is obvious you have somebody up in the attic with you. You woke me up, and I heard them go to the bathroom at six, apart from which there are some strange female garments in there right now.

As you know, I am fairly broadminded, but you have now reached THE BLOODY LIMIT. What will your mother say if she finds out? Could you please see that EVERTHING is <u>back to normal</u> by the time I get home this evening, and that you are <u>the only one</u> in the house. No questions asked.

Dad

The Rosalinda Young Authors Competition

Undated

Hi there!

Have you ever wanted to be an AUTHOR? Have you ever written anything cool you would like to see IN PRINT?

Do you have a Short Story, Poetry, an Exciting Personal Diary, Fine Letters, a Script for Radio or TV? A whole Novel? Or even a Good Idea for a Story Line?

And are you under twenty?

If so, ROSALINDA PRESS may be able to help you…

We have always tried to encourage young authors, and this year we plan to publish THREE first starts by young people…

If you have a manuscript that you think is really good - send it in!

We would be happy to see it… and give you advice about PUBLISHING… if we really see merit in your work

But, please, enclose a large stamped addressed envelope, so that we can return it in good shape

WHY NOT TRY IT! But please, only things that you have worked on really carefully, nothing slap-dash…

NO anonymous submissions, either!

(This initiative is supported by the Teckley Town Arts Council).

The Vicar Complains Again

21ˢᵗ June, 1992

Dear Mr. Price,

As you know, we have been neighbours for many years and have set an example of good relations in the parish. Personal privacy is also part off our local creed and I would not presume to comment on what happens your side of the hedge.

However, Nora was again distressed by a happening last night, when she went out into the garden to feed the peacock. Apparently a casual glance up at your loft conversion window revealed your son Alistair embracing a somewhat unclothed young lady.

Knowing the boy's parents, I have little doubt that such personal contact was within an appropriate Christian context, and we no longer live in the middle ages. But we would much appreciate it if a discreet veil, as it were, could be drawn over such activities, either by getting them to close the curtains or put the light out. Nora gets upset. God bless you.

    Regards,

    Frederic Thorpe.

P.S. Your cat has now obviously been thrust through the hedge twice when our peacock was out. I presume this is one of Alistair's silly pranks and I would be grateful if he would stop it. The poor creature panics and squawks.

... *And William Replies*

Undated

Dear Vicar,

Just a word of apology for the apparition in the window. Alistair did indeed have a friend staying in the house, but I doubt whether anything untoward happened. I know Alistair sometimes fools around with his mother's dressmaking bust, draping it in what he imagines to be a humorous fashion. Are you sure Nora got it right?

As far as Pinkey is concerned, she is very independent, and finds her own way around.

Yours,

W. P.

DIARY – *Father and Son*

22ⁿᵈ June, 1992

It's true. Doris Boxer is actually living in the loft conversion. My God. Decided that the best thing to do in the circumstances was, at long last, to have a one-to-one talk with Alistair. She could be there indefinitely. We can't go on like this. I haven't seen much of the lady yet, but I hear her moving about, and it's clear from the fridge that she eats like a navvy, almost like Alistair. No mention of a contribution, but perhaps that will make evicting her a bit easier. Knowing that she seems to be engaged in theatrical work most evenings, I asked him to drink German lager in the garden. It was the surest way.

I must say the evening air was delightful; a darkening carpet of moist greenery underfoot; the fading sheen of the sky setting off the complex tracery of our large rose bush. I must trim it a bit when I remember. All quiet next door. When we were nicely settled in the Sunshine deckchairs, I began by outlining the naturally changing relationship between father and son, as one ages and the other matures. Literature contains many fine examples of this. Turgenev's "Fathers and Sons", for example. The return of the prodigal in the Bible... Apposite, too, were Lord Chesterfield's famous letters to his son.

In his middling years the parent looks for calm, security, backed perhaps by a little late success, while the youngster is more concerned with starting a career, competing with peers, intense glandular-generated pleasures, and having lots of fun. I thought it apposite to mention Lord Chesterfield's famous hope that his offspring's passion for a somewhat dubious female should not arise above his waist. Complications usually ensued.

Alistair was already sipping his second can of beer, and said he heartily agreed about the glandular bit. As for a career, there was no need to rush things, he still had two years to go at the Poly, and would decide closer to the time, like everyone else.

I went on to impress on him the importance of serious study, and the need for careful accounting in personal affairs. For example, was a never-never agreement on a second hand motor cycle wise? Alistair said the machine was handy for "shifting birds" and launched into some sort of theory about lifetime accumulation, inheritance and taxation. After a while I began to suspect he was trying to work out how much I would be worth when I died.

By the time we got onto Doris, the boy was, I think, on his sixth can of beer and definitely not at his most lucid. I regretted having offered him alcohol in the first place. I told him that the presence of Miss Boxer was placing ever greater strains on family relations, and things could only get worse if she stayed. The neighbours were already talking, and God forbid that his mother should ever find out. When he started singing some awful jingles about Eskimo maidens and a thing called Shadrack's Shag Shack I realised it was hopeless, and ushered him inside. I suspect Nora was listening behind the hedge, anyway.

Actually I had to help him to get to bed.

And that's how it all ended.

Some Bad News for Maisie

25ᵗʰ June, 1992

Dear Maisie,

I thought I'd write you a nice newsy letter instead of trying to tell you things over the phone. At £2 a minute it's hopeless. In fact some good news, but some pretty bad as well.

Let me get the disaster over first. We've been subject to some nasty nocturnal incursions. Last Thurs. or Friday a lugubrious squad of slugs came through the vicarage hedge and (I'm afraid) absolutely ravaged your chrysanthemums along the border. I would guess that Nora put down a nice Christian repellent which drove them to graze here. Anyway, I doused them with a bucket of warm Dettol, which finished them off, but the border looks pretty ropy. The Rev. really is the limit. Last year it was Celia's pet rabbits.

Alistair is in the wars again. He now tells me he failed his maths and economics and will have to retake them in Sept. So no summer job. He says he has a letter ready to post to you (I haven't seen it). He's acquired another girl-friend whom I don't think you'd approve of, but they come and go, don't they. He is maturing fast.

Pinkey is definitely fatter, so you had better let me know where you want her to have the litter. She can't have them under the wardrobe in our bedroom again. The mewing last time was torture. You may also be distressed to hear that Mrs. Porter did get re-elected to the church committee.

Re domestic matters, I thought it would be rather nice

if we freshened up the front bedroom, so I shall reveal my nefarious intent: repaint the woodwork in a light blue eggshell, and re-paper the ceiling. I can get some fine, heavily embossed paper at a discount through Wilkinson's Bromley branch.

You will be delighted to hear that I am getting rid of the caravan, it's too small now that Alistair is grown up. The noise from the next plot was ghastly when we were there last time. More news on that front when we get a sale. It should bring in quite a bit.

Lastly, I wanted to ask you again about the dedication for my autobiography. First I thought simply "To Maisie and Alistair", but can you suggest something a bit more imaginative? Do let me know about the spoons.

   Love,

    William

Maisie Gets Worked up Again

4*th July, 1992*

Dear William,

I can't ring you about this because when I get on the phone to you the whole house is agog (they're paying for it, aren't they). Not to mention Mummy. But really, all I can say, despite trying to be a good Anglican, is – you d-n fool! I just got your last letter.

<u>Of course I didn't bring the bl-dy spoons to Australia</u>, let alone the teapot! I would have told you if I had!!! Have you and Mrs. Wrangle looked everywhere? But how could they have got out of the cabinet? I bet Alistair took them to the poly for one of his daft conjuring shows, and lost them. Like he did with the doilies. I presume there was no break-in, or even you would have told me. So what happened? Leaving the front door ajar again, too lazy to take your key?

Anyway, please get the insurance claim in straight away. The sentimental value is lost, but we can probably get some <u>money</u> for them. You will have to get the police to make a report.

Please keep me right up to date on what is happening. And why hasn't Alistair written?

Fondest love,

M.

P.S. With £3,000 worth of family heirlooms missing, I'm afraid I can't get up much interest about the cat getting herself pregnant. Congratulations on your autobiography. I hope it does us some good. We need it.

Rosalinda Publishers Write to Alistair

30th July, 1992

Re: YOUNG AUTHORS COMPETITION

Dear Alistair,

Thank you for your entry for our "Young Authors" competition. We appreciate your desire to follow in your father's footsteps as a published writer, though our House has, regrettably, been unable to accept any of his manuscripts.

Your outline was vivid in conception, but unfortunately not publishable.

We return your work herewith, and suggest that you press on with your plans to pass your school certificate examination in English. A grasp of basic grammar and spelling would greatly improve your chances.

All good wishes in your creative endeavours.

Yours sincerely,

Mildred Brace

SHE DONE HER BIT

(Alistair's entry for the Rosalinda Young Author's Competition)
by Alistair Price, (Resident 17, Acacia Crescent, Teckley)

This woman, Gloria, is a reelly warm and attractive woman, and the idea behind this reelly exciting novel is to show how bad she was done by, but how she came out like a saint in the end. Gloria is from a poor district in a ropey town (like say Blackbern), she is iliterate, she haven't got no job, and she is also a mother of three kids with no father to keep them, and all the sort of problems of the younger generation. And she's only a bit over 20. She got herself hooked on drugs, because her brother was a pusher, and she wanted to help him sell his stuff, out of the kindness of her heart. She had a criminal record for the cops was always having a go at her, especially when she was with the boys in a lane behind the fish and chip shop. But she never had a chance in life, and her father (as far as her mum could remember) was a black sailor from Jamaica. But underneath it all she had a lovely nature as a child, and it was all mucked up by exploitation and her family not having no money. The problem was, her mum worked on Piccadilly, and did not have much time for her, like. When she was a girl Gloria hated rough games and kept a little rabbit.

The hero, Fred, also lives in Blackbern, in the same district, akchually, but at first they don't know one another. He is 62, much older than Gloria, but he had a tough time when he was young (I'll think of something) but he ends up by being queer and canaballistic, like, together. But underneath he's a good bloke. I done an excellent write-up of the first scene, when you see him in his gas-lit cellar (he wouldn't have no electricity down there) with damp glissening on the old brick walls, eating some suspicious-looking meat for supper. Anyway, one evening he meets Gloria by chance in the lane behind the fish and chip shop, and since they have both had a bad evening, and didn't get no one, they got talking.

Well, they start meeting regular, and a few things happen, but the main thing is that he falls in love with her, and thinks he can trust her. One night he invites her to supper, in the kitchen, and after they had it (the supper I mean), he decides to break the news about hisself, so he says, Did you like the supper, oh yes, she says, I always liked irish stew with lamb, that was no lamb, he says, so what was it then, she says, it was lovely and tender. It was boiled boys bum, he says, I don't think he could have been more than fifteen, that's why it was so nice. So she screams and wants to fetch up and says, you're the dreaded man-eating monster of Blackbern, the cops have been after you for years. He looks absolutely grusome, and she thinks he is going to butcher her, but then he starts to weep, and she has pity on him, and they decide to do therapy on one another for drugs and kanabal homosexuallity, Fred got a book about it from the library. Then she starts getting all she wants from him (physical, like) and don't need no more boys.

Then they get a local council grant and set up a furnishing business, and get rich, like, but just as they are getting to the end of their saikiatric treatment, the police get on both their trails for not declaring VAT in the shop. At the last minute Gloria wins a family holiday to the Costa del Sol, and when they get there they use up there savings to buy plane tickets to South America to start a new life, and they all fly off together into the sunset. With the three kids.

Alistair Price

Maisie Gives Instructions

31ˢᵗ *July, 1992*

Dear William,

I just got another letter from you. They're coming thick and fast now, so I suppose it's bad conscience, apart from the spoons. You don't have to tell me everything is OK if it isn't, I know you both like the back of my hand, and I can guess the sort of mess you've got yourselves into. Piles of dirty dishes, stale food all over the place, the garden going to pot, Alistair having parties every night and Charlie French getting you down to the Goat and Garter all the time.

PLEASE don't do anything more in the garden (except cut the lawn) without asking. You'll poison the earth and the whole thing will be transformed into a desert, like the bl-dy Sahara. I wonder why (of all things) you wanted to have the front bedroom ceiling re-papered? I've been trying to get you to paint the kitchen for years. And why didn't you ask me about the caravan before? If you want to sell something like that you sell it in the spring, not at the end of the summer!

Things have got a bit safer here now that we've had some rain. Eric's house is beautifully situated, very quiet, and the kangaroos aren't any trouble, you can see them hopping through the woodland, and there is a tame koala bear in the garden. Which reminds me, don't worry about Pinkey, I should be home before it happens.

The main problem here is Mummy's blood pressure, poor thing. She thinks it's the years of worry she had with Dad. But I think the eucalyptus vapours have got something to do with it. Why didn't you say anything more about the spoons? I would like to know what's happening with the insurance. William, it came as an awful shock, but every cloud has its "silver lining". If we buy something really nice with the insurance money, all will be forgotten and forgiven. Since you started your literary "career" you haven't given Alistair nearly enough attention. Any sign of a nice girl yet? No letter from him, of course. How can he do it to his own Mother? I couldn't.

Well, that's about all for the present. But please let me know what's going ON.

>Your loving Wife and Mother,
>
>Maisie

Carmarthen Caravans Responds

7th August, 1992

Dear Mr. Price,

Thank you for your letter of the 2nd Sept regarding the sale of your caravan, which vehicle we have now inspected. We can appreciate the care which your wife and yourself have lavished on it, transforming it literally into a little palace on wheels. I agree that the interior is very comfie. However, leakage from the chemical toilet has caused corrosion to the springs, and one of the tyres is flat. A horse has kicked in a rear panel, we had some trouble with them wandering in, but as you know Carmarthen Caravans does not take responsibility for vehicles parked here.

So on receiving your instructions we put it in our Caravans for Sale list, together with the parking place, at a good price (£1200 or near offer) including our 18% commission plus VAT. I enclose an agreement which you need to read and sign. Prices are a bit higher in the spring, if you prefer to wait.

In anticipation of your early reply,

Yours Sincerely,

M. Seldon,
Carmarthen Caravans Ltd.

Mr. Boxer Once More

10ᵗʰ August, 1992

Dear William,

I was delited to learn that you gave Doris a nice room in your house. She told me she came to an agreement about the rent with your son, Alistair, to help him pay off his motorbike. So we're all happy! It is reelly great to see young people help one another in these hard times. It is very handy for her because she has got a job for a season of acting, and she hopes it will be extended to next year. I'm sure her talents will see her through. And she enjoys being in a genuine family atmosfere, like her late mother (my dear sister).

I must ask you again about the Publisher's Advance you owe us. Bristol Channel Publications would be grateful for your most urgent attention to this matter. I would like to point out that on your signature my firm took on big financial undertakings as regarding preparation of the book, and we naturally expect these costs to be got back at an early stage, if not before. An immediate down payment of £2,000, as per contract, is essential.

Some of our regular clients have found it more convenient to pay in cash, and if you wanted to do it that way Mr. Phipps or myself could easily come up and collect the sum in person. In any case, a meeting would be useful to discuss the publicity. We would be reluctant to call in a professional debt collector as yet, and hope it will not be necessary.

With warmest regards and all best wishes for your creative efforts,

>Yours faithfully,

>Henry Boxer

Can Eric Help?

13th August, 1992

Dear Eric,

Another letter to you at work, for obvious reasons. To come straight to the point – I haven't been able to raise the few thousand quid, and the chances don't look good, without going to money lenders who would want equity anyway. Do you think you could chip in? Without anyone knowing, of course. I hope to sell the caravan, but that will not be enough, and the money will not come through in time anyway. The bank has let me down, because Alistair borrowed from them for his motorbike. Also, there's nothing valuable in the house to pawn! It would be a tragedy if the venture fell through. The publishers want payment now. If you can manage something, please cable it through to Acct. No. 464646 at the COOP Bank, 84, Teckley High Street.

The other thing is, it would be best if Maisie could stay out with you as long as possible. Apart from this business of the spoons, I am having a bit of trouble with Alistair and his girl friend, who has moved into the loft conversion. He's threatened to quit the poly if I try and throw her out. For Christ's sake don't tell Maisie, but let me know if she says anything about coming back here. Some hints about staying an extra few weeks might be useful.

Please help with the money if you can.

All the best,

William.

Eat a Friend!

14th August 1992

Dear Mr. Franklin,

I am delighted to inform you that since we last communicated a prestigious publishing House has accepted my autobiography on advantageous terms. Nevertheless I attach considerable importance to my ongoing association with Rosalinda, and have not signed an exclusive agreement with anyone to cover all my writing. I hope you will be able to respond favourably to yet another potentially lucrative proposal.

"EAT A FRIEND!" [Outline]

Ecology is now the rage, and my idea fits the new "green politics". This is not only a work of literature but also a social treatise of considerable originality. Have you ever thought of the economic and ecological problems caused by the disposal of corpses (human beings, cats, dogs and other household pets) and the consequent waste of meat? I am convinced that a reorientation of public attitudes towards the consumption of recently dead protein could be socially beneficial. There is no reason why people should not eat their own pets, or indeed relatives, when the night has fallen on tender personal associations.

Or for that matter, human flesh of unknown provenance. In nature, many species gladly eat their young, if the latter cannot get away fast enough. And who knows what goes into a tin of catfood? Other cats, from the third world? I am sure that the average human loin would be absolutely indistinguishable from a piece of pork, apart from the shape, which could be disguised by careful processing. Another problem is the growing number of pets (as society gets richer), and pensioners (i.e. potential corpses) viz-a-viz the working population.

The main theses of this treatise would therefore be: a) the healthy role of cannibalism in primitive human society, as a source of sustenance, b) current economic benefits, with costings, c) the problems of re-orientating public attitudes from an early age including possible curricular innovations in schools, a press campaign for young adults, so that they could modify attitudes towards parents yet living, etc., d) some moral aspects, what Jesus, Mohammed, Moses, Buddha, said, e) a concluding section entitled "Towards a more nutrient-efficient society?"

It might, for example, be eminently reasonable for the government to introduce a scheme giving pensioners the right to a down-payment on their own carcasses, to be spent while they are still alive. The sum might be enough to keep them in, say, shoes or warm underwear for some time. Families that did not wish to consume their own members or pets could dispose of them for state-approved sums. Public reactions could also be favourably influenced by modifications of the tax system. Then there are important considerations of social prestige. The corpses of well-known public figures could acquire significant financial potential. For instance: how much a plate of freshly deceased Princess Margaret bring at a fund-raising dinner? Prominent individuals could, of course, allot the takings from their corpses to appropriate charities. I am sure I could think of a number of persons in my own family whose parts could be sold with "relative" indifference, if nicely served.

William Price

Rosalinda Press Once More

28th August 1992

Dear Mr. Price,

We have received your "Eat a Friend!" outline, but to be brutally frank, Mr. Franklin thought it palpably ridiculous. In fact, he suggests that if this was intended as a serious submission you may be in need of psychiatric help. A number of our less successful authors have indeed undergone such treatment, and some of them have actually managed to stop writing altogether. As Mr. Franklin put it, meaning-less scribble is often best forgotten.

He has again indicated that on the basis of all you have shown us so far we see no hope of cooperation. Furthermore, an Alistair Price of your address submitted an outline for our Young Writers' competition which also contained a distinct canabalistic element. Does it run in the family?

I would suggest yet again that you find a sympathetic agent, or stop writing.

I am glad you were able to place your autobiography: it will no doubt make interesting reading for some middle-aged folk in South Wales.

Yours sincerely.

Mildred Brace

P.S. Our Accountant, who saw your letter by chance, thought that the administrative costs of handling corpses would in any event be prohibitive.

Alistair Despairs – a note

20th August, 1992

Dad, I MUST have a word with you tonight, when you get back from work. I'll be back about seven. I've got a big problem, Doris is pregnant. What can we do?

A.

To Alistair at Auntie Florrie's

21st August, 1992

Dear Alistair,

I got your note about Doris this morning, and I have only just managed to find out where you are. Not very convenient either, and Auntie Florrie has no phone. In any case, PANICKING will not help. And if anyone has to go, it's Doris. There's hardly any room for you at Auntie Florrie's anyway, she has to let her rooms to lodgers. Would you PLEASE COME HOME WITHOUT ANY FURTHER BUGGERING ABOUT? You can sleep in the spare bedroom. You started this mess, come and help me sort it out.

More problems with Doris. When I got home from work last night there was a hell of a noise upstairs – she had got some VERY rowdy friends in to play cards and booze. She said they were part of the cast from "Hamlet", but they didn't look very theatrical to me. It was more like Jamaica Inn on a wild night. And God knows what they were smoking. Fortunately, she had to leave for a performance, and they all went with her. Where's she working anyway? This just can't go on.

Please get back BEFORE YOUR MOTHER FINDS OUT. You know how news travels around here, especially with Nora Thorpe peering over the hedge.

Dad

Another Nice Letter to Maisie

22nd *August, 1992*

Dear Maisie,

Thank you for your letter. This is just to say that everything is fine here, so DON'T worry. Just have confidence in your utterly reliable spouse. The minor problems I mentioned can all be sorted out with a little time and patience.

I must say, that as the years go by I find myself increasingly indifferent to material things. Literary pursuits are a marvellous release from the tedium of suburban living. My writing, though little understood at our family hearth, performs precisely that function. Though it will one day, I hope, also enable us to enjoy a somewhat more luxurious life style, and move further from the main London railway line.

The main thing at present is for you to have a nice restful time in the "Antipodes"., with some travelling around, perhaps. A pity to leave without seeing Ayer's Rock, for instance, or the Great Barrier Reef. I understand you do not have to dive underwater to enjoy it.

One tiny bit of news – they found poor Miss Crosby wandering down London Road again with a carrier bag of clothes in her hand. She told the police she wanted to get out into the countryside because she'd had psychic warning of another nuclear attack. Pitiful, really.

On the brighter side, I had a nice letter from Mr. Runch at Head Office. He remembered the dress you wore at the dinner and asked me to pass on his best wishes. He is taking a very keen interest in my sales.

I have been in touch with the insurance company. The police advised me to keep an eye on local pawn shops, sometimes inexperienced thieves try and sell things locally. Alistair's out at present, amazing where he gets the energy from.

    Love,

        William

From Head Office, Wilkinson's Furnishings
20th August, 1992

Dear Price,

I'm afraid this is the kind of letter I don't like writing, especially to a senior member of the Wilkinson sales team. Your Branch Manager, Mr. Whitby, and I have been going through the branch quarterly figures, and he thought it would be better if I wrote to you personally as Area Manager.

I recall that when we met at the firm's last annual Xmas dinner everything seemed to be fine, with both you and Mrs. Price in excellent form. Unfortunately, since then your sales effort on the actual floor seems to have deteriorated badly.

Mr. Whitby's figures show that your sales have recently fallen by 28%, though the shop has been doing better than ever. And apart from the mix-up with Mr. Harrison's puffy armchair, which kept the office here busy for two days, we are now trying to sort out the Costarella De Luxe three-piece suite Model 328A you were supposed to order for Miss Yardely-Spence. As you know, she got the Da Costa Comfort bed-settee, with a painfully inappropriate Bridal Gift bottle of champagne. She is in her late seventies and arthritic. We understand she has already complained to the Consumer Protection service. At least two customers have returned pages of your typescripts secreted in the drawers of items purchased. No respectable firm can tolerate this.

Also there is the memo you wrote about the Wilkinson Creative Prizes. As you know, we already have the Young Eagle's Sales Award (two tickets to Wimbledon Tennis matches) and the Middle Manager's Trophy (a winter weekend for two in Torquay). If you got your sales back up to their former level you would be in the running for the Trophy. Your proposal that the firm should start an annual Prose and Poetry Prize could only have been a joke.

We look forward to a marked uplift in your sales performance, so as to avoid discussing your future with the Firm. Our sales positions are highly desirable and we have no difficulty in filling them.

> Yours sincerely,
>
> David Runch

PS (Handwritten) *William, for God's sake pull yourself together and get your figures up! Remember, they'll always find grounds for redundancies in this shithouse! In fact, I'm looking for something better myself. All the best. D.*

Part III

Charlie French Makes a Suggestion

Undated

Dear William,

We haven't seen you at the Goat and Garter for weeks, what with Maisie not here, we thought you was sure to turn up. Anyway, here I am with the Mrs. on holiday in Gower, same old place as you comes to. It's pissing down again, so I thought I'd write a letter to pass the time a bit.

I had a gander at your caravan, like you asked. It looks a bit bashed up – a horse or something have tried to kick the door in. But you could get a fair old price for it. A thou. Perhaps.

I haven't seen you since I went to the Cocked Hat Club in Erdington, have I? They started a Special Businessman's Lunch Show (eleven quid inclusive) on the dance floor. Its called "Dial 999" with a stripper called Belinda Cruise. After the main course they rolls a Post Office telephone booth out. Busty Belinda comes on and squeezes inside it. It's a tight fit, and her cleft sort of gets caught in the middle of the folding door. I think they put the door on special.

Then she dials 999 and starts taking off her knickers. The phone is amplified, so you can hear what she says. She tells the operator (a guy with a real sexy voice) that she needs urgent attention. After a bit it turns out she's a raving nympho who just escaped from the local loony bin. She gets nakeder and nakeder. By the time she hangs the phone up all her clothes is off, apart from a G-string with a big Post Office sticker on her bottom.

At that moment the operator from the Telephone Exchange comes on to handle the emergency hisself. Belinda throws herself at him and grabs him, but then two medics in white coats rushes in and tries to grab <u>her</u>. They all runs between the tables shouting at her to stop, and everybody haves a bloody good laugh. Then the Disk Jockey plays "I put a nickel in the telephone" and Belinda takes the applause. Then she puts on a frilly apron (nothing else), and helps hand out the jelly desserts and sells raffle tickets. She also does a show called the Greek Lamp, but I haven't seen that. They say two men gets electric shocks when they tries to switch her on.

You ought to go and see it, its just got to be closed down, dead cert. The owner of the joint has been in trouble before, they say. We'll be here for another two weeks. Let me know if I can help selling the cara, I'll put in a good word for you. All the best,

    Yours,

        Charlie.

A Letter to a Solicitor

25th *August, 1992*

PERSONAL AND CONFIDENTIAL

Dear Mr. Goldstone,

It has been some years since I was in touch with you, though I still regard your firm as our family solicitor. I would be grateful for your comment on the following highly confidential matter.

Some weeks ago my son Alistair started an association with a certain Miss Doris Boxer, and eventually offered her accommodation in our loft conversion (which they subsequently shared). I have reason to believe that Miss Boxer cultivated a common-wife relationship with my son, and she has informed him that as a result of his intimate attentions she has become pregnant. She claims an emotional attachment and is pressing him to marry her. She is an actress and at present earns money from theatrical engagements.

As if this were not enough, she told Alistair that she has been to the Citizen's Advice Bureau and by virtue of residence in our house has what they call security of tenure. I learned indirectly that she has actually paid my son rent to help him with certain debts. In any case she simply refuses to move out. Fortunately, my wife is abroad, but a disconcerting situation awaits her on her return – unless I can do something about it.

I would be grateful for your preliminary assessment of Miss Boxer's residential and parental rights. What can I do? Could the police be brought in to evict her, if necessary?

Yours sincerely,

William Price

Eric Backs Off

28th August, 1992

Dear William,

Thanks for your letter. Sorry, chukka, there's no way I can let you have any money at present. They've just told me that the foundations of our house are going and it's got to be shored up. I've hardly got enough money for a glass of beer. But I told you to be careful, didn't I? The Bristol Channel Press must be one of these 'vanity' publishers who publish at the author's expense. Some of them are real crooks. What did you sign? Try your bank manager, again. You've been with them for years.

Sorry to hear about the bother with Alistair's sheila. You really never know what these kids are going to do next, do you? Our John got himself poxed up last year, but I didn't say anything to Conny. (Keep that under your hat).

I've got one bit of good news for you, though. I spoke to Maisie about the spoons, and I believe she is over the worst of it. Why don't you butter her up a bit and promise her a nice fur coat when the insurance money comes through? In fact, that's what she might secretly prefer.

As far as I know, she has no plans for returning home yet, and may even stay on for Xmas. I hope you can get the money.

All the best.

Eric

Neighbourly Interest

Undated

Dear Mr. Price,

I do not wish to cause you worry at a time when you lack the moral support of Mrs. Price, but did you know that two men who looked like thieves were prowling round the back of your house while you were at work this afternoon? Nora saw them and she thinks your house is under surveillance. It might be worth you contacting the Neighbourhood Watch officer at the police station to find out whether they suspect anything. The nice houses around here certainly attract burglars.

Do pass on our warmest regards to your wife when you next write. We miss her greatly at St. Stephen's, and hope she will be back soon.

Yours sincerely,

Frederick Thorpe

More Legal Matters

2nd September, 1992

Dear Mr. Price,

Thank you for your letter of the 25th August. Of course, I well remember our contacts in the past.

I cannot advise you fully without knowing a great deal more about the situation. However, in legal terms I can be slightly reassuring. Some young ladies are imaginative about possible pregnancies, especially if there is something to be gained by it. There is not much you can do until your grandchild is actually on the delivery table, and even then your son could (though at some legal cost) deny paternity. Miss Boxer may well have had other relevant intimate associations. On the other hand, the social situation might be a little unpleasant.

I cannot say much about the accommodation problem either, except that security of tenure is usually based on specific conditions which Miss Boxer does not seem to have fulfilled, as she would only appear to be a temporary lodger in your residence. However, proving this and getting a court order for eviction might be tedious, and would certainly cost you more than this letter. Her circumstances and the parency of the child would have to be taken into account. Has your son given her any undertaking in writing? He has, of course, taken rent, which is worrying.

The situation is not easy, but there is no point in crossing bridges before you reach them. Many domestic situations resolve themselves on an amicable basis. What I would suggest is that (after due consultation with your wife) you sit down and have a quiet talk with Miss Boxer, pointing out the difficulties, and quietly asking her to go. You might be agreeably surprised by her response.

I look forward to hearing from you as matters evolve.

Yours sincerely,

Cyril Goldstone

DIARY – *Tea with Doris*

5th September, 1992

My God, an afternoon to remember.

When I got the letter from Goldstone I thought the best thing would be to have a civilized talk with Miss Boxer and try and call her bluff. She might not be pregnant at all. I would tell her we needed the loft for 'other purposes', though Alistair is still at his Aunties's. We can't go on like this.

As it was, events took an unexpected turn. I reckoned Doris would be in the house this afternoon, if not actually in bed. Just after four I called up and invited her down to tea. She yoo-hooed and said yes. As a matter of fact, I had bought scones, a jar of clotted cream and a Dundee cake in anticipation. She appeared a few minutes later with her hair down, dressed in Alistair's jazzy, bum-length dressing gown, and, I suspected, very little else. I put the tray on our Wallingham Sedate coffee table, in front of the three-piece suite. To my consternation she insisted on sharing the settee with me. I was just pouring the second of two cups, when she leaned sideways, looked longingly into my eyes, and ran her hand inside my left loin. The teapot shook wildly, some tea splashed out, and I fear I have ruined Maisie's lace tray-cloth. She says tea stains never fade.

I put the pot down, and moving away a bit, cleared my throat. I asked her, in an attempt at a thespian theme, how she interpreted Orphelia. It was the first thing that came into my mind. "Ain't there nothing more interesting to talk about than that old Shakespeare, William?" she said, or words to that effect. "Alistair never wastes time on things like that!" Then she suddenly heaved herself onto me, her ample bosom pressing up against my chin. Alistair's dressing gown slipped open to the waist, revealing the bare cleft. My legs rose involuntarily as she pressed me back, and I kicked the coffee table, causing all the tea things, including the Dundee cake, to cascade onto the carpet.

It was a dramatic moment. Had circumstances been different, I would certainly have responded in a fulsome manner. Maisie never did anything exciting like that, even in her most womanly years. Doris had just got her hand past my waistband, in the initial stages of what she doubtless hoped would be a voluptuous grope, when, thank God, the door bell rang. It was the man from the Gas Board come to read the meter.

Doris must have thought that the front door was unlocked, because she dashed upstairs, and that was the end of our afternoon tea. The first thing I did when the gasman had gone was to check whether anyone could have seen us. The curtains were, of course, drawn back, but I think most of the activity was safely below the level of the sill.

Obviously, she'll try it on again when we are alone in the house, and the complications are obvious. I am sure people are beginning to talk about her, anyway. Nora Thorpe doesn't miss much, and yesterday the newsagent's boy smiled furtively when he caught sight of me in the shop.

I've got to get Alistair back PBQ, so at least there's someone else around. Perhaps we can persuade her to go into the YWCA. Or something

William Turns to Eric Again

10th September, 1992

Dear Eric,

Thank you for your letter. Sorry you can't help with the money. I'll have to try the COOP bank again. I was glad to hear that M. is calming down. You might just mention that the price of Georgian silver is at rock bottom, and the dent in the pot (which she knows about) could reduce its value further. By the way, not much hope from the insurance company – I stopped paying the premiums last year.

Just between the two of us, this problem with Alistair's girlfriend is getting worse. She's still here and now she says she's pregnant by him. She looked in her middle twenties when I first saw her, but close sightings in a dressing gown have convinced me that she's pressing thirty, years older than Alistair. She must have dazzled him, poor kid. She says she has theatrical engagements in London and knew Laurence Olivier. You should see the underwear she leaves in the bathroom. Maisie never wore anything so scimpy. She made a pass at me when we were having tea yesterday, and God knows what is going to happen next. I suspect Alistair's almost stopped going to the poly. He'll be out on his arse next.

Anyway, I wonder whether you could do me another favour? He has panicked and gone to stay at Florrie's. You were always his "favourite uncle", and a note or even phone call from you, suggesting he should come home, could tip the balance. I thought you could bribe him with an offer of a holiday in Australia next year, I'll pay the fare if it comes to anything. I'll need his help on the spot to oust Doris. Otherwise she can claim unlawful eviction, or something. Thank God for my success on the publishing front, despite the demands for money. At least I've got that to look forward to.

Yours,

William

Alistair's Solution

Undated

Dear Dad,

I got your note. Things going reely well here, Auntie Florry is easy to live with cos she's stone deaf. And I've got some good news for you at last. Uncle Eric phoned last night and invited me to Oz next year if you pay the fare! Wow! Secondly, I had a talk with Doris yesterday. She's a good sort, really, and she told me over a beer that she won't insist on having the baby if I am not sure of my feelings, and from what she heard she isn't sure she would like Mum.

SO she would consider going through with an aborshon, but she is a hard-working girl with no money in her pocket, so after all the upset and hospital she would expect something good like a de luxe holiday, with her poor cousin from Barry, so it would be a cruise for the two of them in the Caribbean or somewhere exotic. Dad, it looks as if we can get ourselves out of this problem for two or three thousand quid. So could you do the readies? I could pay you back bit by bit.

Not a word to Mum, of course. Auntie Florrie's expecting another lodger, so I will probably be back this weekend. Get the fridge stocked. A.

Mr. Boxer's New Proposal

15th September 1992

Dear Mr. Price,

We note that further to our letter of the 10th August and several telephone calls no money has been sent to cover numerus expenses run up under your Publishing Agreement as we requested. Our costs and financial under-takings so far run to three thousand one hundred and twenty one pounds and eight pence (to include photocopying), in addition to the Publisher's Advance you haven't yet paid. It is urgent that the matter should be settled. In view of the financial pressures on our House we have consulted a well-known London firm of debt collectors, who should be in touch with you soon.

It may be of interest to you to know that some genwine authors, after signing a firm Publishing Agreement like you done, have trod the path of success with the help of a second mortgage on their house or a loan from a finance company. It would seem that raising a small sum like this on your highly desirable residence should not be a problem. Then we could get the debt collectors to hold off.

My colleague Mr. Phipps has suggested that it might be helpful to have another meeting at your house when you could make a cash down-payment. Clearly, any debt collector's fees would have to be added to our bill, so an early settlement would be advantageous for you.

Would you please confirm that Friday, 26th September would be satisfactory for us to come about one o'clock.

Yours sincerely,

Henry Boxer

DIARY – *Watery Surprises*

20ᵗʰ September, 1992

A most unexpected "aquatic" day. About half past six, after I got home, I was having a quiet glass of sherry and a cigar in the bath, trying to think out a few solutions. I suppose the Vicar of Wakefield did something similar on occasions. I enjoy a nice soak, with a smoke and a drink, when Maisie's not around. Alistair was doing himself a snack in the kitchen (he's back from his Auntie Florrie's) and Doris was upstairs. There was no change in the domestic situation, at least everything seemed calm.

Suddenly there was a bloody great crash – it was the front door bursting open, and as I found later, the force actually tore the latch from the frame. A man's voice shouted "OK, it's the police! Everyone stay where they are!" Alistair dropped some crockery in the kitchen. Heavy feet pounding upstairs and a terrible shriek in the loft conversion. Some fool broke a window. Then a police siren in the Crescent, and cars pulling up outside. More shouting and a commotion on the stairs. Somebody yelled "It's a drug bust. Upstairs!"

Before I had time to get out of the water, let alone dry myself, the bathroom door also burst open, and in rushed Doris, screaming, with her black negligée all torn. She was trying to get away from a policewoman (it was Sergeant Copplestone, who took my statement after the theft) and two young constables. The bathroom is tiny and in a second Doris had slipped on the wet floor and joined me in my soapy ablutions. She couldn't stop herself. Policewoman Copplestone, a massive creature, slipped as well, and cantilevered in on top of us. Massive convulsions, screeches, and great swooshes of water. Just imagine.

When we got out the Officer in charge gave us towels and insisted that everyone went out and stood on the back lawn while they searched the premises. "Police regulations", and it was a nice evening, wasn't it. My protestations were (in the set phrase) of no avail. They gave me the large "Maisie and William" bath towel we got as a wedding present. God knows what people in the crescent thought, they must have seen a lot of it from their back gardens. Inevitably, Nora Thorpe was out on her stepladder, and even Miss Crosby peered through the hedge.

The police searched the house for an hour, making a terrible mess clearing drawers and cupboards, but they didn't find anything. Doris Boxer was the person they were most interested in, but when she got over the shock she started to make up to one of the constables. Obviously he would not have been averse to closer contact, had he not been on duty. The officer in charge was obviously disappointed they hadn't found anything, but expressed quiet surprise that a respectable couple like Maisie and myself should have someone like Doris as a lodger. He was, as it happened, a member of the St. Stephen's congregation himself. Surely we could have found someone more congenial? He politely regretted the ruination of a fine cigar.

They took Doris away to the station for further questioning, and she hasn't come back yet. They didn't seem interested in Alistair. Smoking is one of the few things he doesn't do. It's frightened the shit out of him again, though. If they keep Doris inside, our lodger problem will be solved. Hope riseth ever.

As soon as they had gone the vicar dropped in to see that everything was all right (in other words, Nora sent him around to snoop). Thank God Maisie's out of it.

The sitting room ceiling is ruined, it's right under the bathroom. Jack Matlock will have to come in again.

P.S. Doris has just got back triumphant. Apparently, they've released her without charge.

A Letter of Explanation

22nd September, 1992

Dear Maisie,

I would certainly not have agreed to take a reverse charges call from Australia if I had known you were going to make a scene literally across the world. They rang back to say that the advised cost was nearly eighteen pounds, and I can tell you that when the bill comes I'm not paying for that. The phone bills are astronomic as it is.

I was appalled to hear that Nora Thorpe had actually telephoned you with a lurid account about the police visit, and your Mother expects me to believe she read my letters to Eric by accident!! I'm sure that whenever she scents trouble she goes through everyone's pockets like a hoover. He should have kept them in the office, where they were sent.

It just shows how distorted things can get. There were only THREE police cars, and the "crowd" outside was only three or four. The police didn't find ANYTHING, and Miss Boxer was released without charge. She may not be quite our type, but basically she's a good-natured girl, and nobody's perfect. Remember the time Alistair burnt the curtains. I've got some cardboard over the kitchen window, so that the rain doesn't get in, and Jack Matlock will be re-glazing it. Whatever Nora said there is only a small patch of wet on the living room ceiling and Jack will do that as well.

I still think it would be wrong for you to come back just now, there is nothing you can do anyway. Miss Boxer's matrimonial plans are not clear, but I doubt whether

Alistair will actually marry her. In any case the rent she pays him is welcome. I'm sure this business will all be sorted out in a few days. I am definitely NOT proposing to take out a second mortgage on the house.

Love, W.

P.S. <u>All</u> the towels have been <u>laundered</u>. Alistair's long-awaited letter enclosed.

Alistair Writes to his Mum

Hello, Mum!

Sorry I have been a bit slow writing about things. I've had my hands full with exams. No need to get upset about the raid, everything's OK now. Doris is a good sort, really. Dad's been reel cool, and all the damage is being repaired. Sorry you were annoyed by Dad's letters to Uncle Eric. Gran shouldn't have shown them to you. By the way, I think we may get into the local paper this week, they don't have drug raids that often in Acacia! Dad's been on the phone to try and stop it. But if we're in, you'll be famous!

I won't be taking a job this summer, cos I've got to take a couple of extra exams, so I might be a bit tight, like, with the readies. Any chance of Gran chipping in? What's she do with it all, anyway? That's just between the two of us.

Dad's done a lot of cleaning up and the place looks reely nice. I've promised to cut the lawn. Pinkey's fatter than ever. Watch out for roos, they kick something wicked. Regards to everyone, particularly Gran!

  Love,

    Alistair

ST. STEPHEN'S PARISH NEWSLETTER

Editor: Mrs. Nora Thorpe.

EXCERPTS FROM THE REV. F. THORPE'S SUNDAY SERMON.

29th September, 1992

I have taken as our text today, dear friends, our Lord's injunction, "Love thy neighbour as thyself" because this precept is so frequently needed in our everyday lives. One might think, in the little world encompassed by our parish boundary, that neighbourly love might be superfluous, even intrusive. Around us a modest opulence is the rule, and most of us have the wherewithal to live happy lives, in a materialistic sense, without thinking about what goes on next door, or across the street.

But even in circumstances such as ours, things may not be what they seem. And often, it is only by the merest chance that we glimpse the unhappiness that beshrouds many a neighbour's hearth...

Neighbours have existed as long as society, indeed, they *are* society. Not only may they have problems of their own, but they may *be* a problem for others. Come to think of it, even we, as good Christians, know literally nothing about Jesus's neighbours, and what they had to put up with. But we can imagine a few things. Jesus was not a desert nomad (like, if I dare say so, Mohammed) and almost certainly lived in crowded urban conditions. We know that he attracted unpopularity when, at the tender age of twelve, he was arguing the toss with Rabbis at the local synagogue. I wonder whether any of them went around to his parents to complain? He must have been a somewhat contentious youngster.

Then there was his carpentry business, a noisy profession, with banging and sawing, not to mention the delivery of planks. The modern parallel would be the garage repair shop, or noisy youths on motor bikes. Yes, we all know the situation. Even Jesus must have caused some grumbling among those living close by.

I would also imagine that his disciples could be a problem. What would you think if, for example, your next-door neighbour suddenly brought twelve grown men back for a meal late at night, just when you were dropping off to sleep? All the wine and argument? Thumps behind the wall? And no indoor sanitation? Especially if you knew that some of them were unemployed, and had problems with the police?...

That's what living next door to Jesus might genuinely have meant. So if, in this day and age, your neighbour is no paragon, but an ordinary sort of person, with many failings, a particular measure of charitable love is called for. Occasions arise constantly, I could mention one or two in my own little orbit, even now.

What is the Christian response? Not a confrontation in the heat of the moment, of course, as that could only make things worse. One possibility is a charitable word of advice, by telephone or letter, a call across the garden fence, with benign intent, openly expressed. A public prayer for the individual concerned, in one's own church? That could provoke more embarrassment than contrition, at least if a name were mentioned. I myself think a silent, communal prayer, each of us thinking of someone known to be in need of divine guidance, is the most Christian –

...Let us spend a moment together in silent prayer...

News from Australia

5th *October, 1992*

Dear William,

Now you know, I gather Maisie told you. All hell broke loose here after your vicar's wife phoned. And how that old cow got into my briefcase, I don't know. Come to think of it, she may have been at it for ages. She's been on the prowl since the spoons disappeared. Miss Sodding Marples isn't in it. Maisie almost went berserk and demanded to phone you straight away. Thank God I reversed the charges! Anyway, dear Gran is now having another burst of her favourite pastime – high blood pressure, and is lying out in the garden. At least it's quiet.

You may be relieved to know that Maisie thinks it would be unwise to leave her, so she's staying on here for the time being. That may make things a bit easier for you.

Alistair seems keen to come, when you can get the money for his ticket. I think you've got a fine youngster there. I will let you know if Maisie looks like making a move. Any news about the spoons?

    Yours,

    Eric

DIARY – *An Evening at the Cocked Hat*

12*th* October, 1992

All has been exposed, and my God, there was plenty of it.

Charlie French is back from holiday. He phoned last night and asked me to go and see Belinda Cruise at the Cocked Hat. He'd heard about the drug bust. "After all you've gone through ... Maisie'll be back soon, make the most of it... They does the Greek Lamp on Thursday nights..." And so on.

The place was packed, but Charlie got us one of the front tables. The lights were turned down, and the Disk Jockey played "The Entry of the Queen of Sheba" – a bit of Handel to add class. A moment later Belinda, done up as a Greek goddess standard lamp, was wheeled in, standing on a sort of plinth with castors. Actually, we used to sell something similar at Wilkinson's for about thirty seven pounds fifty. You couldn't see her head, though, as it was covered by an enormous lampshade, with pictures of nude Greeks, like a frieze on the Parthenon. It occurred to me that the person who designed it had a good grasp of the needs of the Erdington public. Belinda's robe was short and semi-transparent, suggesting interesting things to come. A yell of delight went up from the audience.

I don't know what made me turn my head at that moment, but I could have sworn I saw Fred Thorpe standing at the back, with a muffler covering the lower part of his face. But the shadowy figure quickly disappeared, and I could not be sure. Nora, I thought, wouldn't have tolerated it, anyway.

When Belinda was in place they plugged her flex into a wall plug, and a cheerful glow illuminated the frieze. Everyone cheered again. The music changed to a sexy Greek folk song, and she gradually allowed her robe to slip down, assuming various classic poses and revealing ample contours. She was certainly more developed than Maisie when in the same age-group. When the robe reached her attractive abdomen she cavorted, pulled a little cord, and the lampshade suddenly dropped down to her waist, forming an unexpected miniskirt. The robe fell away completely, revealing graceful lower limbs. But when I looked back up at her face, I found I was observing the features of none other than Doris Boxer. Somehow, the thought had flashed through my mind when I read Charlie French's letter. A floor show would suit Doris better than the role of Orphelia.

She had, of course, seen me through the Pantheon frieze. She handed her robe to an electrician, and as soon as she was free of the wires she skipped over to our table. In an instant, to my intense embarrassment, she had settled on my knee, in the full glare of the club spotlight. She hugged me and implanted a lingering kiss on my cheek, exclaiming loudly, "We should have done that before, shouldn't we?" Everybody laughed, and a man at the next table, who was clearly the worse for drink, offered me his congratulations.

After that unforgettable moment Doris did some highly suggestive solo dancing, and when the music stopped announced that she would be taking donations for the Bristol Channel Old People's Home in Penarth. Could everyone please be as generous as possible....

Charlie and I left soon after. Doris is now abed in the loft conversion and Alistair is in the spare room. God knows what's going to happen next. I am almost tempted to ask Fred Thorpe for spiritual guidance. I feel I've completely lost control of the situation.

The Solicitor Again

16th October, 1992

Dear Mr. Price,

I am sorry I was not in the office to take your call earlier today, but the gist of your questions has been passed on to me.

The fact that Miss Boxer was involved in some sort of one-off melée with the police, without significant damage, nuisance or bodily harm, would not normally affect any tenancy rights she may or may not have. In any case, the fact that the police released her without charge would imply that she committed no offence.

But if this sort of situation hopefully occurs several times, we might be able to consider legal action for nuisance. Please keep me up to date on developments.

Yours sincerely,

Cyril Goldstone

DIARY – *A Visit to the Library*

20ᵗʰ October, 1992

Melodrama is not a genre that I enjoy, and I try to keep it out of my writing. Yet "Woe is me" is a refrain which keeps ringing in my ears. I have taken up arms against a sea of troubles, but at this moment in time (3am on the 20th October) my frail craft looks like floundering in a sea of debt, family disintegration and creative failure. This is what happens when an honest author takes publishers at their face value.

Yesterday evening, after work, I went down to the public library to have another flick through the Artists' and Writers' Handbook. Teddy Drage was on the reference desk. He used to work for a publisher himself. When I requested the Yearbook he asked me why I needed it, and I told him about Bristol Channel. It all just sort of gushed out. He was horrified, and immediately confirmed what Eric had said – Bristol Channel are 'vanity' publishers who charge naïve, would-be authors incredible sums by promising to bring their work out. This lot is clearly unscrupulous, and fearfully expensive. I have put myself in the thrall of small-time crooks.

The whole thing has a horrible simplicity. Why didn't I see it before? Has the tough world of high-street commerce taught me nothing? I thought there was, indeed, something fishy about the reverse Publisher's Advance, but the joy which overcame me at the prospect of publication blinded me to all dangers. Perhaps Maisie was right after all: I should have stuck to selling furniture.

Teddy suggested getting into touch with a solicitor, or emigrating, or both. I don't know *what* will happen if

Boxer and Co. come up to the house, as they did before. Even if I'm not here, Doris would let them in. And my chances of getting rid of *her* without any trouble look slimmer than ever.

For the moment I'm having a quiet cup of tea in the kitchen, before the peacock starts. Perhaps I'll feel better when it gets light. The prospect of temporary exile to Australia, with Maisie and her mother, is not at all appealing.

Another Police Operation

25th October, 1992

TECKLEY ARGUS

"Popular Venue closed by Police."

There was uproar among customers at the Cocked Hat Inn, Erdington, last night when they found themselves involved in a police raid with no less than fifteen officers. Despite the pandemonium and protests from disappointed clients, the police made two arrests – the proprietor (Mr. Gus Johnston) and a striptease dancer (who performed under the pseudonym of Belinda Cruise). Mr. Johnston is a popular figure locally, and Miss Cruise had acquired some renown for her rendering of erotic scenes at "business" lunches and dinners. Mr. Johnston's licence has been suspended, and the establishment temporarily closed.

The police were tight-lipped, but before being bundled into the police car Miss Cruise, dressed in a Greek robe, her hair dishevelled, shouted that the police had a "downer" on her, because some of the same officers went to see her off-duty, and thought she might "pull the plug" on them. She claimed she was only an ordinary working girl who did "the best she could" for herself. Police sergeant woman Copplestone subsequently divulged exclusively to the Argus that the proprietor has been charged with keeping a disorderly house, and Miss Cruise with indecent exposure, assaulting a policeman, hindering the police in the course of their duty, using foul language in public, selling bogus lottery tickets and wasting police time. Other charges may be pending.

It was alleged earlier this year that the Cocked Hat was also a centre for the distribution of "soft" drugs, but no firm evidence was found to back this. Miss Cruise's performances had been going on for some weeks, and had become progressively more explicit. According to Police Sergeant-woman Copplestone a number of complaints had been received from the public, including one from a local church council, after the vicar had called in for his evening pint.

Argus readers who frequented the Cocked Hat may draw some consolation from the fact that so popular a venue is unlikely to be closed for long. We understand that negotiations had already been started for a change of management and possible reopening under a new name. Watch these pages.

Nora Thorpe writes to the Teckley Argus

27ᵗʰ October, 1992

Dear Sir,

As a regular reader of your admirable newspaper I was a surprised at an inaccuracy which slipped into your yesterday's article the precipitous closure of the Cocked Hat public house, Erdington, with which my husband, the Reverend Frederick Thorpe, was slightly involved.

Your reporter stated that "a local vicar called in for his evening pint" implying that my husband was a regular visitor, and also drank alcohol beverages.

To avert possible misunderstanding, I would like it to be known that the Reverend Thorpe had never before entered the establishment, and called in purely by chance, as an old age pensioner who lived nearby was not at home to receive him. The Reverend Thorpe decided to wait a while at the Cocked Hat, not realising what was going on in the Club Room there. He has assured me that he only ordered a glass of tomato juice with a little Worcester sauce, and left quickly. I hope you will find it possible to publish this correction, as men in public life must be scrupulous about their activities.

I remain, Sir,

    Yours faithfully,

        Nora Thorpe

William Triumphans

TECKLEY ARGUS   10ᵗʰ November, 1992

"Dramatic Police Ambush at Teckley Home"

Swindlers Caught Red-handed

A dramatic and highly successful police ambush took place yesterday in broad daylight at the Acacia Crescent home of Mr. William Price, furniture salesman, after Mr. Price courageously tipped the police off regarding an anticipated visit by two men sought countrywide for swindling and possible drug-peddling activities. Henry Boxer and Wallace Phipps of Penarth, South Wales, (with several aliases) were taken into custody and are currently being questioned at Teckley Central Police Station. We understand that charges will be preferred shortly. A third associate, Miss Doris Boxer, has already been remanded in custody on other charges. Arrests of other associates may follow.

Criminal Intent

As reported in the last issue of the Argus Miss Boxer worked as a stripper under the show name of Belinda Cruise at the Cocked Hat, that is, until it was closed. She was detained on charges including indecent exposure. Yesterday's arrests suggest that the gang may have chosen the Cocked Hat as a possible centre for drug-peddling, if it had not actually started. Mr. Price's timely information prevented this happening. According to police comment, the trio ran a marijuana drug-peddling ring, the substances being stored at a publishing depot in Penarth and distributed as needed through strippers in Kent clubs. Each stripper was expected to develop her own clientele, sometimes under the guise of collecting money for charity.

Along with this the gang operated a bogus publishing agency called "The Bristol Channel Press". It was designed to attract gullible writers who were desperate to get published. The technique involved gaining the confidence of people who never expected to be cheated, involving them in excessive donations to charities for impoverished authors or in fanciful publishing projects. The victims were threatened with legal action if they did not pay promised contributions or promised costs. In a few cases contributors' homes were used as safe lodgings for the gang's criminal associates. Mr. Price contacted Bristol Channel Press on account of his genuine literary interests, but soon found he was under pressure to pay huge, fictitious publishing costs, and was landed with an unwanted lodger in the shapely form of Miss Boxer.

The police ambush was skilfully organised, with Mr. Price's active participation. "It was obvious after the first police raid on our house, and Miss Boxer's arrest", he told us, quoting Hamlet, "that something was very wrong in the state of Denmark". He was galvanised into action by a threatening letter from Boxer and Phipps saying they were coming up to his house to claim a substantial sum of money in cash. Although they must have known of the earlier police raid at Acacia, when Miss Boxer was detained but not charged, they were probably unaware of her arrest at the Cocked Hat. Certainly Boxer and Phipps anticipated no problems when they went after their victim in the Crescent yesterday. Mr. Price, however, had taken their letter along to the police station, and agreed to a police snatch at his own fireside. Though suffering some facial injury in the scuffle which ensued, he is delighted at the outcome. "I would do it again tomorrow, if need be," he told us.

A Fair Cop

The day started quietly, like any other in Acacia Crescent, with Mr. Price going out to work. Mrs. Price is currently on holiday in Australia. Neighbours around No. 17 were not aware of a police presence. Miss Jane Crosby, a pensioner 74 years young and the Price's next-door neighbour, had spent most of the morning in front of the house trying to persuade her cat to come down from the Japanese cherry. "I think he's got fur fleas from the Price's She," she declared, "and I wanted to powder him. But he's a devil if he thinks you are trying to catch hold on him. I was out there trying to have him most of the morning. I'm not nosey, but I must say a lot of people went in next door, unusual really. Alistair opened the door, he doesn't go to the Poly every day. There were two men with a council van, two who looked like door-to-door salesmen, a plumber, two from the Electric and a lad who was delivering one of them pizzas. That must have been for Alistair. When she's home Maisie bakes herself, and never lets that kind of rubbish in the house. The funny thing was that no one came out, except the pizza boy. William came home himself at twelve. But I got the cat down by then, so I went in."

Mrs. Nora Thorpe, who lives in the Vicarage on the other side of the Price residence, told us she spent most of the morning in the kitchen with her daughter Celia, making rock cakes for the Church Tea. "I could not see what was happening in the Crescent," she said, "but about one o'clock when I was cleaning the front windows I did see two gentlemen arrive, one middle aged, and one younger. Mr. Price met them on the doorstep. Soon after they went inside I thought I heard shouting. Then two police vans drew up, and some uniformed officers rushed in. Eventually the front door burst open, and the two business gents were pushed out, surrounded by other men I hadn't seen before, plus the policemen. I noticed that one of the businessmen had a black eye, and Mr. Price's nose was bleeding. Some of the blood had got onto his shirt. If it was one of the 100% cotton ones Maisie bought him for Xmas she'll murder him. They all piled into the vans and drove off. It was quiet again after that. We were all left wondering what had happened.

Of course, it wasn't the first time the police had been to the house, you know. There was what they call a "drug bust" there a few days ago, but they didn't find anything. It was all to do with that dreadful girl who lived in the loft conversion. I can't imagine why William let her in. But he's obviously very brave, and we've got a lot to thank him for."

(See "An Unassuming Hero", page 7 of this issue)

A Mystery Solved

15th November 1992

(A letter from the Police Sergeant Woman Copplestone to William Price)

Dear Mr. Price,

May I refer to the loss of household valuables regarding which you made a statement on the 23rd August of this year.

It would appear that articles closely fitting the description have now been recovered. We would be greatful if you could call in at the station as soon as convenient to make a formal identification, and collect the articles. Please telephone in advance any working day between 9 and 5, and ask for the Lost and Found Officer.

The successful solution of cases such as these is always a source of pride in the Force, especially where excellent relations have been maintained with members of the public through the Neighbourhood Watch throughout.

    Signed

        Police Sergeant Woman Copplestone.

Good News for Maisie

17th November, 1992

Dear Maisie,

I bet you were glad to get my phone call yesterday! All's well that ends well. I enclose a cutting from the Teckley Argus, as promised, with all the gory details that I didn't have time to give you over the phone. Please note that the shirt was NOT one of my cotton ones, Nora Thorpe always gets things wrong, and what business is it of hers anyway. The Boxers are well and truly off the map, as a matter of fact the police have already been to collect Doris's things.

I went down to the police station this morning and got the silver back. Apart from an extra dent in the teapot, it's all fine. I bet you're wondering how they found it! It was Miss Crosby's evil deed. We think she must have wandered in when I was seeing the Boxers off after they came for lunch, and she took it from the cabinet. She's going downhill fast, poor thing. Perhaps she wanted to bury it with her own stuff before the nuclear holocaust. The only thing was, she forgot to tell me about it. Anyway, they picked her up outside the bus station at midnight on Tuesday, with the silver and a few belongings in plastic bags. She said she was trying to get away again before hostilities started. I think an old people's home is the only answer there.

Everything is OK at home, so don't worry. Jack Matlock will be doing the other ceiling, and Mrs. Wrangle is still coming in. Whitby was delighted that the shop was mentioned in the Argus, and (believe it or not) hopes the story might attract a few customers. Hope riseth ever.

I trust everything is going smoothly your end, your Mother can calm down a bit now. Go on having a quiet, really relaxed holiday. There's no reason why you shouldn't stay into the New Year, if you want to. Will write again soon. Alistair has promised to enclose his own letter.

Love, William.

Alistair Straightens Out

Hi, Mum,

Its me again. Just to confirm that everything Dad says is right, no waffle this time. The great news is that Doris was joking, and you ain't going to be a Granma, not quite yet, anyway! (Joke) After she got pinched she admitted there was nothing in the pregnancy story. They say she might get a year for indecent exposure, even if she wasn't in on the drug dealing, so it would have been a bit inconvenient to have a baby inside. Pity, though she was a bundle of laughs.

You'll be glad to hear I've got an incredible new girl friend. And you know her! Its Celia from next door. She's a bit older than me (15 years), but she's a rave and I've started dating her. A really reliable sort, she's got to be, cos she's a single mother (Big secret). Thats why the wicked vicar wont let her live in the house, and pays the rent on a flat for her in Croydon. She's got over her drink problem and she's says she's really into stable family relationships. Their coming back into fashion. She says her little boy needs the extra care because he's a darky, and you know how much racial prejudiss there is around. Well, I told her, the colour of his skin dont worry me, I think he's cute, and I'll be his dad. I promised to get him a toy motorbike or something for Xmas. Celia thinks his fathers in prison, but she's not sure, because he dont write, but its better to have him out of the way, isnt it?

What I said about the readies still holds good, and I wonder whether you managed to have a word about it with Gran. Relax, and have a great time.

Love, Alistair.

More Motherly Worries

25 November, 1992

Dear William,

I expect you will be surprised to get this by express post, but I did not want to say anything over the phone, because it's not the sort of thing I want to be known in the family, but I've got to tell you I was PROSTRATED by the note Alistair sent with your last letter, as if we haven't had enough disasters already.

I really don't know how you could allow it all to go on under your very nose without noticing. Now it's that Celia Thorpe. OK, she's entirely wrong for him, and far too old, but did you do anything to try and stop it? I never heard that she had an illegitimate child. And coloured. It's incredible what goes on in the most respectable houses, even the vicarage, though I must say I always thought Nora was too secretive about that girl. I suppose if you asked me, which nobody did, I would have said she didn't say much because of Celia's life style, and living away in Croydon, without a job, she was a bit ashamed of her. Well, if Alistair is stuck on her we've got a big job on our plate. It could well cause unpleasantness on the church council, too. Does Nora know about it, do you think? If she thinks the whole thing happened because of him, she's not going to be very pleased is she? She may think it is demeaning for Celia. Though I suppose it all would have had to come out some time.

Anyway, I have now definitely decided to come home as soon as I can get the ticket endorsed, Otherwise it'll be just drift, drift. I'll let you know the exact time of arrival by telephone, can you get time off to meet us? Or send Alistair? By the way, I've asked Mummy to come back with me, and stay for a few months, she can have the spare bedroom, that's one of the advantages of the loft conversion, a good job I thought of it. I think she will have a calming influence. I get the impression that Alistair is fond of her.

I'm afraid this letter is a bit of a mess, but I must say, William, that I really am quite upset.

Love,

        Maisie

P.S. I hope you were being accurate, and that the "dent" was only a small one. There's no end to it.

Congratulations from on High

25th November, 1992

Dear Mr. Price,

It is not our normal practice to write letters of congratulation for sales effort, particularly when our more senior employees are involved. They know without speling it out that their sales efforts are always appreciated by our Board.

I would, however, as Chief Executive, like to thank you personally for your efforts in obtaining the refurbishing contract for the "Cocked Hat" in Erdington. The new proprietor, Mrs. Alfreda Topley, tells us she admired your arrangements on the sales floor of our High Street branch, and has no hesitation in giving us her custom. Although the jungle decor she requests is a little outside our normal run of activities, we can do it! (Thick bamboo stalks, she believes, have erotic associations which will appeal to younger clients.) You may not be aware that this is the largest contract Wilkinson's has obtained for many years. (Well done, William!)

Apart from the usual commission, you will be pleased to learn (on a strictly confidential basis) that you are currently way ahead for the Middle Management Annual Award (a weekend for two in Torquay). The result will only be announced after the closing date, but there does not seem to be much doubt who's the winner. We are delighted with this turn of events, as no doubt will be you and your Lady Wife. Please keep it quite for the time being, to avoid envy among other staff.

Finally, you may have heard that your Area Manger

Mr. Runch has just left the firm to take up a position elsewhere (I believe as manager of a betting shop in Brixton). Our attractive post will shortly be advertised, and an application from your Good Self would be given serious consideration. Of course, you would not have to move from your current address, if lucky enough to be selected.

Yours faithfully,

        Moira Hempworth, Director

ST. STEPHEN'S PARISH NEWSLETTER

1st December, 1992

Editor: Mrs. Nora Thorpe

"Day by Day"

Members of the congregation, and residents of Garden House in particular will be delighted to hear that Mrs. Maisie Price is shortly expected back from Australia. Mrs. Price will be accompanied by her Mother, who, I am sure, will get the customary warm St. Stephen's welcome. Welcome home, Maisie!

"Major Literary Success."

It is nice to see that happy events coming in clusters. We can congratulate Mrs. Price's husband William on the successful placement in the hands of a fine publisher of his autobiography, *'A Swansea Boyhood'*. The work, it is whispered, contains some lovely vignettes of Mr. Price's life in Wales and of his parents, who by a strange stroke of fate were actually married at St. Stephen's altar nearly half a century ago!.

Mr. Price's creative writing came to the notice of Larehall's Press after his bravery in helping the Police to apprehend some vicious criminals, as parishioners will well remember. We are told that Mr. Topley, a director of the firm, who lives locally, and a fellow Welshman, was intrigued by Mr. Price's public image, and contacted him personally, with this happy outcome. Mr. Price revealed to us that the advance would at least cover the cost of some decoration before Maisie got back. A lesson to us all, I think, in domestic understanding.

It is indeed gratifying to have a literary figure amongst us. Mr. Price has indicated that signed copies of his book will be available for purchase by parishioners when the work appears. I am sure many of us will look forward to reading it.

Mr. and Mrs. Price's son Alistair continues his economics course at Teckley poly. Congratulations to the whole family on this major literary event.

For Sale

Four attractive tabby kittens available in about six weeks at affordable prices.

Ring Alistair, Teckley 777666, evenings.

Printed in the United Kingdom by
Lightning Source UK Ltd., Milton Keynes
140921UK00001B/5/P